PLEX PRESENTS

GET IT HOW YOU LIVE

Can't Stop! Won't Stop! Can't Forget! Won't Forget!

BY BIG GEMO

GET IT HOW YOU LIVE

Copyright 2011 by: Big Gemo & PLEX
Written by: Big Gemo
Edited and Perfected by: PLEX
Cover Design Created by: PLEX & Cedric 'Ckillz' Killings
Cover Graphics by: Cedric 'Ckillz' Killings

This novel is an absolute work of fiction. Any resemblances to real, living or dead establishments, actual events, organizations, or locales are intended to give the fiction a heightened sense of reality and authenticity. Names, characters, places, events, and incidents are products of the author's vast imagination and are fictitiously, as are those fictionalized events and incidents that may seem to involve real people and did not occur or are set in the future.

PLEX PRESENTS BOOKS. Published with permission by BadLand Publishing, LLC
P.O. Box 11623
Riviera Beach, FL 33419-1623
ISBN: 978-0-9825018-5-6
First Edition

Aint Nobody Pen'in Like Us Man!!

Acknowledgements

First and foremost I'd like to thank the Most High for the strength he's given me to move on when I felt like giving up. Thank you God for all of my blessings. To the greatest mom in the world --- Ms. J, I LOVE YOU! Whenever I look back it's you that's always in my corner. I know that I can never pay you back, but the plan is to show you that I understand, you are appreciated. A special thanks to Ms. Gin, TaNesha, TaShara, and Tasnim. Y'all been like family to me, and I love y'all...Chaka, thanks for sticking with Da' Kidd on this one. I got nothing but love for you, Amari and Armani..To my RIDE OR DIE'S – Missy and Danielle – I love y'all both with all of my heart. Thanks for not letting go of what we have..I ain't forget y'all – Scooby and Phats, I love y'all too...To my ace, my nigga, my dawg – Lil' Var. Thanks for always keeping it 100 with yo' boy. I got real love for you, homie. ..Lil' Gemo and Omar, y'all are the best brothers a nigga could ask for. I love y'all both!!...Big shout outs to Ms. Kita, Juanita, and all the homies on 56th Street, Bunny, Ant-Wee, Pooh, Teddy P, Noko, Kel, Marvo, Dirt, PJ, Nuke, Nikkia, Debony, my cousin Jem, C-Jisim, Cory, M-Ray, my lil' cousin Ant, Nard, PaPa, Weezy, Money, C-Walk, Poochie, Pinky, Bo-Jay, Mu-Mu, Zay-1, Money Grip, Piggy, Pooh-Bee, Rochelle, and the realist Arab's in the world (up at BAWA Food Markert), Joe, Mike, Rick and Sammy. Good looking out!!!...Carol City 191, Norwood, Lil'River, Brown Sub, Opa Locka, and the whole Lil' Haiti...My dawgs in the Chain-gang; Bo, Ball, K-1, Bino, KD, Hen, Dre, Neil, Cap, E, Jay, Paypa Chase, G-Baby, Hot Rod, Pee-Wee, Homie Joe, JB, Des, Money Roy, E$, Bling, Big Joe Hollywood, Worm (Blue), PI, Tae, J-Roc, Nard, Disco (30 Row), Head, Zoe, Pitt, Money Mark, Poppa Stoppa, T-Fleezy, Rick Brownlee, Dee, Will, Bolly, Mo, Fresh (Nate), Pop (the realest nigga out of St. Pete), Deuce (Bruce Smith), Jahhead, Tracey & Kim (The Badland Boss Ladies), Ms Tweetie (the Book Diva), and Willie Dutch...A special thanks to Plex for giving a nigga the opportunity to do something big with this here book. I love you man (no homo)...I'ma hustler baby/I just want you to know/It ain't where I've been/but where I'ma about to go/TO THE TOP OF THE WORLD!! RIP James A. Smith AKA Jack Boi, Damian Miller, Pretty Boy, Lil' Mane, Fatz, Lil' Dumbo...I love and miss y'all boys!!! FREE ALL MY DAWGS!! Rah-Rah, Way-Way, Dee, Steve, Var, Von, Mono, Stanka, Fluka, Boss, Lil' Derrick, Sam, Bam,

Monk, Frantz, Serious, Bo-Jit, Niko, Hubba, and OJ Simpson (The Juice)....WE BADLAND FOR LIFE.

OFF THE RULER'S DESK

If you're reading this, it only means that the BADLAND BOOK GANG has done it a muthafuckin' 'gin. Which makes me proud, yet at the same time humbles me. For in all truth, this was never supposed to happen. I was supposed to get consumed by my circumstances and lose all touch of reality. Prison was supposed to reduce me to nothing. Instead, it produced this. A movement fueled by this novel, written by my lil' fool, who never graduated from high school. He was sent off to prison, not to be rehabilitated or refined, but to be warehoused until his release, or killed before he could make it. However, he met me, and now you have this — Get It How You Live — an expression of his hopeless past...a symbolist of our future. For what he was he is no more. Not because the system set up programs to educate and better him. But because he picked up a book – a book of Urban Fiction – and read it! He then dared (challenged) himself to write one of his own. He wrote...he wrote about past experiences that he no longer wishes to reenact. So please don't judge him on "what he writes", but congratulate him on the mere fact "that he writes". Because he could be living it instead of imagining it. So thank you to the reader, for your time and support.

BADLAND PUBLISHING has sold over 10,000 books independently. That is without any paid advertisement, and without any sort of distribution. This is a feat that we are very proud of, yet could not have possibly accomplished without you – our loyal friends and supporters: Seth Ferranti, Willie Dutch, Dwayne Gladden, Steven Polk, Ms. Trina (The Diamond Princess), Debra Harrel, Tracy Davis, Troy Cannon, LaMont Needum, Pam Quigley, Jahhead, and the two hardest working ladies in the publishing game (Tracey and Kim)...Also Skip (my dog Wood), LaLa (his ride or die), and Christopher Ross.

Thank you all so so much!!! Please continue to check www.badlandpub.com for new releases, and continue to order from us via mail (our ordering form is in the back of this book). We appreciate your love and support and take great pleasure in bringing you the best in Urban Literature.

One Love,
PLEX

STREET RULES

IT'S NOT JUST FOR THE LOVE
OF MONEY; ITS FROM LACK OF CHOICES,
AND THE ONLY WAY LEFT TO SURVIVE.

NEVER REALIZING WHEN SCRATCHING OUR
NAMES IN THE WET CONCRETE AS LITTLE
KIDS, THAT THIS WAS OUR TOMBSTONE,
AND WHERE WE WOULD DIE.

BEING 100% REAL TO THE GAME IS ALL I EVER KNEW,
AND OUT OF THE MILLIONS WHO CLAIM TO KEEP IT REAL
TO THE END THEIRS ONLY A FEW.

I GREW UP CHASING MONEY AND FOR
THE LOVE OF DOE THERE'S NO LIMIT TO THE THINGS
I'D DO OR THE THINGS I DID

BUT THAT'S THE LIFE YOU SEE IN MY HOOD,
AND WHAT YOU CAN EXPECT DEALING WITH LITTLE HAITI'S KIDS

I WAS TAUGHT MONEY OVER BITCHES
AND TO ALWAYS LET MY NUTS HANG;
AND WHEN NIGGAS CROSS YOU UP IN THE END,
LET THE GUNS DO THE TALKING AND MAKE THE
STREETS REMEMBER YOUR NAME.

RODERRICK VANN

Part 1NE

"Everyone has insecurities. When you show yourself in the world and display your talents, you naturally stir up all kinds of resentment, envy, and other manifestations of insecurity. This is to be expected..."

— Robert Greene

THE BEGINNING

Chapter 1
Fresh Out

"Inmate Brown," the fat white Correctional Officer called out.

"Right here, CO," BG answered.

"Number?"

"79141-004."

"Date of birth?"

"11-22-84."

"Come with me, Brown."

All eyes were on BG as the fat CO walked him out of the crowded room. It stunk like a high school gym after a hard day's practice as everyone locked inside waited impatiently for their name to be called.

The dirty county jail was no place to house a *real man*. It was cold as fuck, and there was a vicious pack of rats and roaches that would consume your commissary before you ever had a chance to.

The only thing worst than the rats and roaches were the snitches and the CO's. They were two different sets of *fuck-boys* doing the same thing in a different way. One group helped the *crackas* catch you, while the other held you until your day to be crucified.

It was all a part of the game, though. And if you played it long enough you were bound to fall victim to this trap. One's just had to respect it and keep it moving. Whether you're a robber, dope-boy, or a common car thief, you knew that one day you were going to have to pay the piper. So as the old adage goes, *don't do the crime if you can't do the time*.

¢ ¢ ¢

The bright sun hit BG in the eyes and slightly blinded him. It had been a little over a year since he'd last felt the warmth of the Florida sun on his dark-brown skin, and it felt good – not only on his skin, but to be a free man again.

He considered walking over to the property window to collect his belonging, *but fuck that lil' shit*, he said to himself and continued scanning the block for his ride. BG was ready to see his girl – Missy. He had big plans for an unforgettable night with her.

Just as the images of Missy's beautiful naked body played across his mind he spotted his brother's car bend the corner. *Damn!* he said as he watched the 24" Floaters do their thing on the candy apple red Nissan Maxima. The car's windows were limo tinted out, the *Protected by Glock* sticker highly visible.

As soon as BG opened the door he was hit in the face by a heavy cloud of chronic smoke. The scent was sweet, and he could not help but to smile as he took the blunt from his twin brother – LG.

"What's up, boy?" LG said excitedly.

"I'm free, that's what's up!"

LG laughed at his big brother. "Nigga, you act like you been up the road and shit. You ain't did nothin' but a punk-ass year in the county, my nigga."

BG's lungs were full of the potent cannabis when LG's comment came across, causing him to gag and choke. It had been

10

a long time since he'd smoked a real street blunt, and he was really feeling it.

"Boy, you aiight?"

BG had tears in his eyes from coughing so hard. "Yeah...bruh, this... weed... so, some... fi'."

"Nothin' but the best, bruh."

The two rode in silence for a while, Jim Beam's *They For Everybody* beat down low as the Max floated towards LG's crib.

"I'm feelin' this whip, lil' bruh."

LG looked at his brother. "That ain't all you feelin'," he laughed, because BG was *dumb-high* on the passenger side. "But, hey, you know how the kid do."

LG didn't tell BG that he'd gotten the rims and music from Mono for the ultra-low-low, because he didn't want to hear his mouth. BG didn't like buying stolen shit from thieves unless the stolen products were guns, drugs, or *splacks* to go body a nigga in. Anything other than that he would pass on, because stolen shit could be identified and could easily become a problem that he didn't need. Not to mention the fact that he didn't trust or like roguish muthafuckas.

"So whatchu gettin' into tonight?" LG asked.

"Some pussy," BG replied flatly.

The closer they got to home the more his mind surrendered its sobriety to the weed. His thoughts were strongly affected by sexual desires for Missy – the 5'5" 125 pound lady of his life. Missy had an ass like Buffy the Body, nice sexy lips, and a set of eyes to die for. BG was *for real-for real* in love with her, and he had good reasons for feeling the way that he felt.

Missy had rode with him like a champ during his stint in the bing. She wrote him almost daily, and she was there to see him at least twice a week.

Now today he would be giving her a surprise visit. For Missy had no idea that her man was once again free. And that's exactly how BG wanted it. He only hoped that he wasn't the one that would get the surprise – coming home to another nigga hitting his girl.

¢ ¢ ¢

"Yo, bruh… nigga, get yo' mind right, we here." LG brought BG out of his daze.

"Damn, my bad," BG said, shaking his head. "That weed gotta nigga gone… plus that baby on a nigga mind."

"Yo' ass just pussy-whipped, nigga."

"And you're a hater."

"Hater?" LG questioned.

"Yeah, you heard me, a hater."

They both laughed and exited the car. LG had a small apartment in a building on 61st Street and 13th Avenue. BG hated the location and wondered why in the hell did his little brother choose to live in the middle of such a fucked-up hood.

The building was a three story construction with about sixteen apartments on each floor. LG lived on the second floor. His apartment was decked out with top of the line electronics – 54" plasma, PS3, and surround sound.

The living room and bedroom were equipped with leather king-sized sofas and canopy bed, while the big walk-in closet was over capacitated with fresh, new designer wear.

LG was living ghetto fabulous at $550 a month rent, he and his *hood-bitch,* Shara. LG had been loving and shacking-up with Shara since forever. She was 5'6" with long pretty hair and the cute face of a 17 year old – though she was 24. The only thing wrong with Shara was the fact that she was too damn hood. Of course, that's what LG loved most about her – baby was down for her man, and that meant *whatever-whatever.*

"Yo, Shara! You home?" LG yelled.

"LG, don't come home askin' stupid-ass questions… I know you saw my damn car out there!" Shara yelled back, with attitude.

"You let her talk to you like that, bruh?" BG asked his brother, laughing.

"Nigga, fuck you!"

"LG, who you out there talkin' to?" Shara yelled.

"My brutha!"

"BG?" Shara called back. "Who that nigga done told on? I thought he was stretched out."

LG fell out laughing.

"Bitch, I ain't told on nobody!" BG fired back, because the shit wasn't funny to him. "Bruh, you better check yo' people...bitch got me fucked up."

Shara came out of the bedroom in her tiny booty-shorts, bra, and house slippers. "BG, I ain't gon' be all them bitches. I was just playin' witcha ass, anyway."

"Well don't play with no nigga like that," BG continued, "What's up witcha, though?"

"I'm good, nigga, how 'bout you?"

"Straight, now that a nigga out."

"Shiid, yo' ass woulda still been waitin' outside the county, fuckin' with yo' sorry-ass brutha. I had to remind 'im to pick yo' ass up."

"Oh, I'm sorry now, huh?" LG asked.

"Nigga, do–not–start, ookay?" Shara stated, and gave LG *one more look.*

"Damn, Shara, what's up with yo' big-booty-ass sista?" BG asked.

"Nigga, you done bumped yo' muthafuckin' head... 'cause I'm not tryna beat that tired-ass bitch of yours ass."

"You're a hater, just like yo' man."

"Whatever, nigga." Shara gave him the hand. "Ain't nobody hardly hatin' on you."

"Then what they call it now?" BG asked her.

"Saving Missy from a ass-whippin', that's what I call it," Shara shot back.

BG knew that it wasn't any winning with the talking-ass ghetto queen, so he just left it alone. "Bruh, you got some more of that weed?"

"Nah, but we can cop some and hit the liquor store after you wash that county jail off yo' ass and come up outta them blue county scrubs, my nigga." LG went into the closet and pulled out a fresh Coogi fit. "Here man, wash yo' ass."

BG took the fit and hit the shower. After which he lotioned up and jumped Dade County sharp. It felt damn good to be out, and he was feeling himself, Coogi fresh as he came back into the living room.

"Nigga, you think you cute," Shara said, eyeing her man's older brother.

"Nah, you think I'm cute, hater," BG said as he walked out of the door.

¢ ¢ ¢

Over in Little Haiti on 59th Street and 3rd Avenue, JackBoy, Bo-Jit, and Teddy P all sat on the corner smoking weed and watching the flow of traffic that streamed in and out of the trap.

This was an everyday thing for the young fools from Dade County, where it was Trap or Die; and some trapped and still died. Never realizing that life and the pleasures that existed within its realms encompassed far more than the false sense of security that drugs and guns provided; and surely included a little more than cheap sex, death or imprisonment before age 24.

"What's up with ya, boy?" Bo-Jit asked JackBoy.

"The kid should be out by now."

"He comin' through or what?"

"I ain't holla at kid yet, but I know he gon' holla, though."

"Dog, I'm ready to get this money. Straight up! I ain't for all this waitin' shit."

"Patience, kid..." JackBoy hit the weed and repeated. "Patience."

"Yeah, dog, stop bein' greedy." Teddy spoke for the first time.

"Greedy? Nigga, who the fuck was talkin' to you anyway?" Bo-Jit shot back.

JackBoy looked at his two partners and started laughing. The two of them always seemed to bump heads in one way or another. "Y'all boys chill out. We gon' be straight, feel me? The kid out now and we 'bout to make this power move, together... feel me?"

"Dog, a nigga just hungry, that's all."

As JackBoy was about to respond to Bo-Jit's last comment his cell phone went off. He had Rick Ross' *Hustlin* for his ring tone. After peeping the number on his screen he knew exactly who it was.

"Yo! Is this my nigga right here?" JackBoy asked excitedly.

"Boy, JackBizzism, what's up?"

"You, kid, you what's up." JackBoy was happy as hell to be capping with his man.

"We was just talkin' 'bout you, kid."

"Well I hope it was some boss shit bein' said."

The two friends had a good laugh at that. JackBoy and BG had known each other their whole lives. They were like brothers, and often stayed at one another's house when they were little snot noses growing up.

"Yo, me and LG 'bout to hit the liquor store and I'll be right in yo' chest."

"Make sure you grab some woods, 'cause we got plenty of pine, ya heard me?"

"You got that."

"One..."

"Hundred."

JackBoy hung up the phone and gave his two men the *haps*. The phone call from BG was what they'd been waiting for.

15

LG had called JackBoy a few days earlier with a message from his brother. BG had a plan, and the plan called for a few good men. Naturally, JackBoy called up Bo-Jit and Teddy P.

Bo-Jit was a wild young Haitian with very fair skin, dread locks, and a mouthful of gold-teeth. He swore by God he was a real ladies' man. Even tagging himself *The Haitian Sensation*.

Teddy P, on the other hand, was cock-eyed and big as a house. In fact, he looked just like Deboe from Ice Cube's movie *Friday*. And he was just as mean and crazy.

"Yo, JB, that look like the twins right there." Bo-Jit pointed at the fresh red Max as it hit the corner.

"Yeah, that's the homies." JackBoy hopped off of his crate. "There them kids go."

LG parked his car on the corner where the trio stood. BG was the first to jump out, dead-fresh, blunt in hand, and a bottle of Grey Goose in the other.

"What's up, y'all boys?" BG slurred.

"We good," the three youths answered almost at once.

LG passed out some cups while JackBoy walked over to his white Ford LTD with *dark-boys* and 23" Spooners on it. The car wasn't flashy, but it was running and it was paid for.

JackBoy came back from his car with a half-ounce of 'dro, just in time to hear his little man *dumb-ass-out.*

"I'm sayin' though, BG, you and LG are *dougie* or whatever, and I'm feelin' the vibe. But, dog, a nigga ain't no groupie. I came out here to talk money," Bo-Jit spoke with assertion.

JackBoy and Teddy P looked at each other like, *yo, can you believe this nigga?* And then quickly turned towards Bo-Jit with more serious looks.

BG peeped the whole scene and finally spoke, "Yo, Jack, what's up witcha man?"

He'd said little, but he thought a lot. While BG was gone for that year in the county, he did a lot of reading and stayed in tight correspondence with his older cousin Gemo – who was serving real time up in Coleman Federal Penitentiary.

The two wrote each other weekly, and with his correspondence Gemo always sent a book title. The best three in BG's mind were Mike Harper's *STREET RAISED: The Beginning*, Robert Green's *THE 48 LAWS OF POWER* and Plex's SERVED: With No Regard. He read and studied those books like they were the Holy Scripture... Now it was time to apply it.

Avoid the unhappy and unlucky, because you can surely die from someone else's misfortune, for emotional states are as infectious as diseases... BG paraphrased Robert Greene's statement in his mind. The dude Bo-Jit was cleary unhappy, and displayed a lot of the characteristics of *Shorty* from *Street Raised* and *Action* from *Served*. Neither were good looks, so he decided to bounce.

"Aye, Bo, my nigga, what a nigga told you, man?" JackBoy finally said.

"What?" Bo-Jit played the nut-role.

"Look, man, I'm fresh out," BG spoke to everyone. "We gon' talk money, but not right now. I'm 'bout to be up."

As BG went to get the keys to the Max from LG, a dark colored car with *dark-boys* on it came creeping up the block.

Everybody except BG started pulling out hammers. From .9mm's to .45's, they were aimed and ready to *Swiss cheese* the unknown vehicle. Murder was on the minds of the gun toting hoodlums, and its evil presence could be felt hovering thick in the air.

The car drew closer, and the tinted window began to roll down. LG gripped his Mac-II a little tighter and prepared to squeeze. JackBoy raised up, and a voice called out from the car.

"Damn, y'all don't fuck with a nigga no more?"

LG looked closer and lowered his weapon. "Chill y'all, that's Rah-Rah."

Everyone lowered their guns and breathed a deep breath of relief. Especially BG and JackBoy. BG hadn't been out a day yet, and was not ready to go back to jail on murder charges. While JackBoy did not want his trap on *A&E's First 48*. The *crackas* would be all over the hood terrorizing the people and running that forensic bullshit. All of that was bad for business, and the trap was his business.

"Nigga, you almost got that shit tore up!" LG yelled.

"What, y'all boys beefin'?" Rah-Rah asked as he got out of the rental.

"Nah, but we woulda been if we woulda fucked around and killed yo' ass," JackBoy said angrily. "Niggas on point 'round here, so don't be comin' through here like that, fool."

"My bad, kid," Rah-Rah said before spotting BG. "Damn kid, what's up?"

"I'm on that Carter 3, Rah-Rah...A Milli, ya feel me?" BG capped.

"I hear you."

"Nah nigga, do you feel me?" BG corrected.

Rah-Rah smiled for the first time and his 32 gold-teeth lit up the block. "I feel you, big homie, I feel you."

"Aiight then...y'all boys be safe out here. I got a lil' business to go handle, so I'll see y'all tomorrow."

"Don't eat too much business, bruh." LG laughed. He knew that the business his brother was going to handle was positioned between Missy's thick thighs.

BG just laughed and gunned the Max down the block, headed for I-95. As he rode he flipped through the disc changer with the remote control.

"I should've known this nigga ain't have no slow grooves," he said to himself.

Finding Tupac's *All Eyes on Me* CD, BG skipped to *Run the Streets* and rode out.

Chapter 2
<u>Daddy's Home</u>

"Bitch-ass-nigga, open the muthafuckin' safe," Lil One whispered to the *vic* as soon as he entered his condo. "If you make *ann* fucked up move I'ma put it in yo' life!"

"Do-do-don't shoot a nigga, playa, please."

Lil One slapped the dude once behind his ear with the large caliber handgun, causing some leakage of blood. He then forced the *sucka* to the master bedroom where he knew the safe was located. Precious had been fucking and sucking information out of the drug dealing lame for the past two weeks. She had also beat him for his spare key and security codes. The one thing that she couldn't come off with was the combo to the safe.

Lil One pushed the dude down before the large picture of a naked woman.

"Well, whatchu waitin' on, fool? You done been out *shonin'* all night, now it's time to break bread."

The dude knew then that Lil One knew about the safe. He also knew that he'd been set up. The only problem was, he partied so hard with so many bitches, he didn't have a clue as to which one could've played him so dirty.

Lil One broke his train of thought with a vicious blow to his head. *Whop!* The blow sounded and sent blood splattering against the wall.

"Look, fool, get that picture down and that safe open."

Just as the dude removed the portrait from its place and began working the safe's dial, a phone started ringing.

"Where that phone at?"

"In my pocket, playa."

Lil One was on pills and heavy lace, so the ringing of the phone didn't just irk the shit out of him, it made him extra-noid.

"Fool, reach in yo' pocket and turn that shit off."

The dude did it and went back to opening the safe. *Click!* It sounded and Lil One pushed the dude aside. The safe was stuffed with money and two kilos of cocaine. Lil One smiled when he saw the little .32 automatic under the bundles of money. Precious had told him that the dude kept a gun in the safe.

Removing a Familiar Line sports bag from the inside of his big Dickie jacket, Lil One started filling it with money and drugs. He could see his *vic* sitting up against the wall where he had pushed him.

He was almost finished emptying the safe when a phone started ringing again. Lil One turned to face the dude. "Didn't I tell yo' ass to cut that shit off?" Before he could answer, *Boom! Boom!* Lil One fired the gun. One slug struck the floor, the other went into dude's leg.

"Aaaaaah!" the *vic* yelled.

"Shut yo' bitch-ass up," Lil One demanded and went into the dude's pocket. The phone was off. "What the fuck?" Lil One patted his own pockets and remembered then that he'd brought his own phone on the lick without turning it off. "My bad, dog."

Dude didn't say anything, he just continued to hold his bleeding leg.

"Yeah?" Lil One answered.

"Boy, what's up?"

"Who the fuck is this?"

"BG, lil' nigga."

"Oh, boy what's up?"

"Shiid, this money. Whatchu doin'?"

"Robbin' this nigga in Miami Lakes. I done shot the nigga and all."

"Nigga, you're crazy!"

"I'm for real," Lil One slurred.

"Yeah, that's the crazy part." BG laughed. "Look, though, my nigga, Daddy's home now, and I'ma need some big fi', my nigga."

"I gotcha, fool, but let me finish what I'm doin' and I'll hit you later on."

"One hundred, my nigga," BG said, laughing and hung up the phone.

BG couldn't believe what he'd just heard. Nor could he stop laughing. He'd known Lil One for almost five years. When Lil One was released from the Feds, Gemo had sent him to holla at BG and BG had looked out for him. Ever since then, whenever Lil One hit for guns or dope, he'd serve BG for the super-low.

BG had love for Lil One, but right now his mind was on Missy. So he downed his cup of Grey Goose and continued towards County Line Road.

¢ ¢ ¢

Missy stepped out of the shower and prepared herself for a night of *Tiny & Toya*. After drying off, she lotioned herself down in cocoa butter. She loved the way it kept her skin soft, smooth and glowing.

"I wonder why BG hasn't called?" Missy questioned herself as she slipped on a pair of pink panties and an oversized T-shirt. "I hope that everything's okay with him."

Missy's thoughts were interrupted by her doorbell.

"Now who is this ringing my bell when I'm ready to watch me some TV and relax?" she asked herself.

The doorbell rang again before she could get there.

"Who is it?" Missy yelled.

"Special delivery, ma'am!" a male voice called from the other side of the door.

Missy opened it and found a delivery man holding flowers and chocolates.

"I'm sorry, sir, but you must have the wrong apartment."

"I'm looking for a Ms. McDonald, does she live here?"

"That's me, but I didn't order this. Who's it from?"

The delivery man chuckled, revealing nice white teeth. "I'm sorry, Ms. McDonald, but I don't read the cards, I just deliver them."

"I guess I'll take them, then."

"Thank you." The man smiled. "Will you please sign here?"

Missy quickly scribbled her name next to the X, took the flowers and candy, and closed her door. This whole ordeal was unexpected. Who could be sending her flowers and candy?

She placed everything on her coffee table and then opened up the card.

Dear Missy,
I am so crazy in love with you...
        Sincerely,
        The Only Man for You

Missy was really thrown now. Maybe BG had gotten LG to place the order for her, Missy thought. "Oh, he's so sweet," she said to herself and picked up the phone to call and thank him.

Wait! her mind screamed. *Girl, what if they are not from him?*

It had to be him, who else would be sending her flowers and chocolates?

Again her thoughts were interrupted by her doorbell.

"I know this better not be anymore flowers or candy," she said as she stumped off towards her front door.

"Girl, who done sent yo' tired-ass flowers?" Keisha asked.

Keisha was Missy's fine-ass, shoning-ass, next door neighbor. She was always in everybody's business, and just happened to be peeking out of her window when the delivery man brought the flowers.

"Girrl, you sho' is all up in mine, *Ms. Nosey,*" Missy said it in good humor, but really meant what she'd said.

"Girl, whatever!" Keisha popped. "You still ain't tellin' me what I wanna know."

"Girl, I don't know...I think BG sent the flowers, but I don't really know. I wanna hit LG and thank him, but if they ain't from his brutha, girl, he gonna kick my ass when he get out."

"Well, if it ain't BG, then it's from whoever else you been givin' the booty to," Keisha said, smelling the roses. "And just in case you ain't know, that makes you a hoe."

"Girl, you're crazy! I'm not givin' up nothing, okay?"

"What-ever...now tell me who ya fuckin', hoe."

"Eat me, bitch," Missy said, and slapped her big juicy ass. "Ain't nobody hitting this, it's all for BG."

"Is that right?" a male voice asked from the doorway.

Both Missy and Keisha turned to find a man standing there.

"BG!" Missy yelled and ran into his arms. "Yo' slick ass! Why you ain't tell me you was getting out?"

"I wanted to surprise you, baby." BG kissed her big pretty lips. "Surprise!"

"Keisha, girl, you can leave now. I'll talk to you later, 'cause my Daddy's home."

Keisha shot Missy *one more look* and headed for the door. "Shiid, I've been kicked outta better places by better people. So y'all can miss Keisha... and don't be makin' all that muthafuckin' noise, 'cause my kids home."

"Bye, Keisha," BG said and walked Missy to the bedroom.

This was the moment that the two lovebirds had been waiting on. BG didn't waste anytime removing the large T-shirt that Missy had been wearing.

The two moved towards the bed, their lips still glued together. BG savored the sweet taste of Missy's tongue as he massaged her apple bottom.

After slowly laying her down he slid her pink panties off. Missy melted under BG's passionate touch. Her love-box began to cream as his kisses left her neck and traveled further down south.

Her nipples... her navel... her hairline... the center of her wetness.

"Oooh, Daddy!" she moaned.

Missy closed her eyes and readied herself for the extreme pleasure that she was about to receive. Tears ran from her eyes as she rocked her hips to the tempo of BG's stiff, wet tongue.

"Oh my God, babe!" Missy sang.

Missy was at the brink of a climax. She gripped the back of BG's head and grinded her pussy against his face.

"Yes! Yes! Yes!" she managed to say before the cum erupted from her clitoris and the shaking began.

BG didn't waste anytime slipping all 10" of his throbbing manhood into Missy's ocean of pleasure. She jumped at first, but he continued to deliver long tender strokes. Sweat poured from both of their bodies.

"I love you, baby," BG whispered in her ear.

Her only response was a pleasureful grunt and a continual gripping from her inner walls. BG was in pure bliss.

"Oh, bay...hit it from the back."

BG stopped mid-stroke and turned her around. *Damn!* he thought, looking at Missy from behind. She had enough ass to eclipse the sun.

"Oh, yeah, bay... yeah, right there," Missy sang as BG found his groove.

In and out… In and out… His tempo began to increase. It had been over a year since he'd felt that *oh-so-good* sensation building up in his loins.

"Missy, baby, I'm 'bout to cum!" BG groaned.

"Then cum on, babe!"

And with great pleasure BG erupted like a violent volcano in Mauna Loa.

¢ ¢ ¢

Back on the block, LG, Teddy P, JackBoy and Bo-Jit were still hanging loose. The corner was their spot and rarely did they leave it.

At twelve o'clock the shifts changed in the trap-house. Shifts ran from twelve to twelve. LG had the night watch, while JackBoy ran the day shift. They pushed crack. Bo-Jit ran both shifts because he dealt in weed and soft. With this system in play the three of them ate, every man earning his keep.

"Man, where the fuck is 50 at?" LG asked no one in particular. He was upset that dude was late for his shift—again!

"I don't know why you ain't fired his ass yet. Shiid, time is money, yo," JackBoy said.

"Patience, man, I'm fuckin' the nigga's sista, whatchu want me to do?"

"Shiid, let her work the sack then."

"No bullshit, I need to." LG laughed. "The way that bitch keep her hand out…but for real, baby gotta mean *head-game* on her."

"Yeaahh?" JackBoy asked, gripping his dick.

"My nigga! That bitch can suck a nail through a 2x4, yo…no bullshit!"

"Letta nigga get the number," JackBoy cracked. "Don't cuff that, kid."

"My nigga, a nigga don't cuff no *rosses*. It's 786-718-6943, yo. But you ain't get that shit from me."

Bo-Jit saved the number in his cell phone as well. After all, *it ain't no fun if the homies can't have none.*

"Y'all boys shot-out, yo." Teddy P laughed. "That's the homie sista, man."

"Nigga, you just sayin' that shit 'cause yo' baby-momma got yo' lovesick-ass pussy-whipped," Bo-Jit shot back.

"I aint' pussy-whipped, yo."

"Then what y'all lovesick niggas call it now?"

"How 'bout I'll whip yo' ass, nigga!" Teddy P was in his feelings.

Bo-Jit laughed. "Funeral homes are big business... I ain't seen a fight in years... niggas killin'," he rapped Plies' song while holding his .40.

"Whatchu sayin', yo?"

"Nah, nigga, what I said."

LG stepped up before shit got too far out of hand. He knew that Teddy P would punch Bo-Jit in his shit. Just like he knew that Bo-Jit would shoot the shit out of Teddy P. "Y'all two chill out, yo... it's the liquor talkin'."

Just as LG had settled the situation, JackBoy spotted 50 walking up the street. It was 12:50 and he was supposed to have been to work damn near an hour ago.

"Damn, yo, where the fuck you been?" LG snapped.

"Had to watch my sista's kids," 50 answered.

"Why you ain't call and tell a nigga somethin'?"

"I did call, yo," 50 explained. "Yo' shit kept goin' straight to voicemail."

"Stop lyin', 50. My phone ain't rung since we been out here."

50 tried to tell LG that he wasn't lying but Bo-Jit cut him off and took him inside to change shifts. He didn't have time to sit around listening to 50 tell lies. They had to count out the bomb and money, and then somebody had to take the day shift worker to the crib.

LG watched as they counted out the money and drugs. He knew he would need some more work to last his worker until morning. He reached into his pocket to get his cell phone but couldn't find it. "Damn!" he said under his breath. "I left my phone in the car with BG."

He felt bad for calling 50 a liar, but he was not about to apologize.

"JB, let me hold yo' phone to call Shara right quick."

JackBoy tossed LG the phone. Shara picked up on the third ring.

"Who this is?"

"Yo' daddy, girl... what's up?"

"Nigga, what-the-fuck-ever... whatchu want?" Shara snapped.

"Fuck is wrong witchu?"

"What nigga?"

LG sighed. "Look, Shara, I need you to —"

Shara cut him smooth off with so much attitude. "Nigga, whatchu need is some muthafuckin' toys! 'Cause you ain't gon' be playin' with me. Nigga, I been callin' yo' muthafuckin' phone all muthafuckin' night! Where the fuck you been? Probably over there fuckin' 50's AIDS having-ass, crack-head sista. But bitch, if ya give me somethin', I'ma kill yo' ass and that bitch! You just a nasty black mutha—"

"Shara!" LG yelled, finally able to get a word in.

"What, nigga?"

"Will you please shut the fuck up! I left my phone in the car with my brutha, and he gone to his girl house."

"Oh," she replied. "So whatchu want?"

"Bring me a stack of each, yo."

"Why you can't come get it yo'self?"

"Bit—" LG caught himself. "Shara, didn't I just tell yo' lazy-ass that my brutha got my car?"

"Oh," she replied again. "So whatchu want, a stack each?"

27

"That's what I said ain't it?" LG was getting tired of Shara's shit.

"Nigga, you ain't gotta be gettin' all slick and shit. 'Cause I'll fuck 'round and don't come at all."

LG sighed. Why did he love this hoodrat, foul-mouthed bitch so much? "Why you always gotta make shit so hard for a nigga?"

"Whatever, boy, I'm on my way. You on 59th right?"

"Where else would I be tellin' you to bring me my shit?"

"I already told yo' ass don't be gettin' muthafuckin' slick, nig—"

LG hung up the phone in Shara's face and gave it back to JackBoy.

¢ ¢ ¢

The trap was jumping. LG was posted up in front of the house when Shara finally bent the corner. 50 had damn near sold Bo-Jit's entire sack.

"Boy, come get this shit outta my car!" Shara yelled before the car had even stopped.

"Look here, yo," LG said when he got to the car. "You gon' stop all this tryin' a nigga, for real."

Shara pulled the two drug bombs out of her little stash spot and handed them to LG. "Boy, ain't nobody hardly tryin' you."

"Whatever, yo. Wait right here, I'ma drop this to 50 and I'ma dip with you."

"Well, ya ass betta hurry up."

LG ran in and counted out the bomb with 50, got a total for the night and ran back out to Shara's Nissan Altima. She was still pouting and cursing like a damn fool, but that was Shara. And for real, that's why LG loved her.

Chapter 3
Keisha's Way

"Wake up, sleepy head," Missy cheerfully sang into BG's ear.

She was about to head off to her job at North Shore Hospital on 95th Street and 12th Avenue.

Missy got up early everyday so that she'd be on time. However after last night's heavy dose of sex, she wasn't in the mood to go to anyone's hospital. She really just wanted to lay up with her man. Of course, the bills had to be paid. And though she knew that BG would look out for her on the money tip, like he always has, she insisted on being independent, which meant working and taking care of herself.

"Mmaann, what time is it?" BG whined.

"7:30."

"What the hell you woke me up for?"

BG had never been an early bird. Even while doing his bid in the county, BG would sleep late into the afternoon.

"Boy, I gotta be to work on time, and I wanted to feed *my man* before I left."

"Girl, who the hell eat this early?"

"I do, BG," Missy whined. "Plus I thought it would be nice to eat together for a change. You've been gone for over a year, bay... this is your *welcome home Daddy breakfast*."

29

"Well, ya ass thought wrong," BG barked and turned away from her.

All he wanted to do was go back to sleep. That and curse her ass out for getting him up so early. Missy knew how BG felt about being disturbed. He'd once told her, "If the damn house ain't on fire, don't bother me!" So in his mind she already knew better. Still, he held his tongue.

"Baby, look..." Missy spoke softly. "I already started, the food is almost ready, so please don't do that."

That did it. BG turned to face his baby. "Aiight, let me get myself together."

"Yeah, do that." Missy frowned. "And make sure you hit that tongue, 'cause bay, yo' breath stank."

"Come here!" BG jumped up and tried to grab her.

"Aaahhh!" Missy screamed as she ran from the room laughing.

¢ ¢ ¢

After a quick but very tasteful breakfast BG went into the bathroom to smoke an early morning blunt. Missy hated the smell of weed, but BG loved the widely cultivated psychoactive herb.

As he burned he thought. His next move had to be made. BG had planned and plotted his entire bid. Now it was time to execute, and timing was everything. He needed to act quickly, because he was financially fucked up. Yet he knew that he couldn't act hastily. In doing so he would betray a lack of control. The 35th law of the 48 Laws taught that one had to become a detective at the right moment.

"Timing," he said to himself as he exited the bathroom.

When he walked into the bedroom Missy had the best after breakfast dessert he'd ever seen waiting for him. She laid there in the bed, naked with her thick legs wide open. A river of syrup ran from her chin to her *love-box*. *Damn!* BG thought as he dove in headfirst. He licked and sapped up every drop of the sweet maple syrup, loving every minute of it.

"Wel-welcome home, Daddddy," Missy moaned as BG found her swollen clit and began to ravish it.

Just as BG lifted her legs and started eating her ass, the phone rang.

"He-hel-hello... uhh!" Missy could barely get her words together with BG's tongue in her rectum.

"Girrrl, no yo' ass not!" Keisha's ghetto-ass yelled into the phone. "Tell that nigga to let the pussy breathe, damn!"

"Ke-isha... wh-what you want? Oooww, boy."

Keisha's pussy thumped a bit on that last note. She'd heard all of the excitement last night through the apartment's thin walls. Now she wasn't just nosey, she was horny.

"Missy, bitch, gimme some milk so these bad-ass kids can have some cereal."

"You, oh shit.... gon' ha-have to-to wait."

"*Hmph*, y'all bitches is too nasty over there. I just—"

Missy hung up the phone in her ear. BG was finished eating ass and was now all the way up in her. She had already came twice and was now on the edge of a third climax. The clock on her wall read 8:10. She had to get to work.

"Ooww, bay... this feel sooo good," she moaned. "But you gotta stop... stop, bay, I gotta get to work. I'ma be late."

I can't believe this bitch! BG thought as he withdrew his dick and watched her big juicy ass bounce as she ran off to the bathroom. *I could've stayed sleep*, he continued to think with a hard dick.

The ringing of the phone broke up his thoughts.

"What?" he answered.

"Damn, nigga!"

"What, Keisha?"

"Is y'all two freaks done over there?"

31

"Is yo' hoodrat-ass just being nosey or do you want somethin'?" BG was sitting there frustrated, with a bad case of the *blue balls*, and didn't feel like fucking around with Keisha's gossipping-ass.

"*Hmph*, nigga, you wouldn't believe what I really want," Keisha sassed. "But *anywho*, I need some milk for my kids."

"You better tell that sorry-ass nigga you got to buy some."

"BG, boy, I'm not gonna even go there with you." Keisha breathed easy. "Can I please get some milk?"

"Yeah, yo." BG sighed.

The two of them sat holding the phone while silence filled the line.

Keisha finally spoke. "Well is you gon' bring it, or yo' butt just gonna hold the phone?"

"What, girl, is you—"

"Please, BG, pleaassee?"

BG sighed. "Yeah, yo... you got that."

He hung up before the bitch decided to beg up on some cereal, too. BG hated begging-ass, nosey-ass, trifling-ass people. And Keisha was exactly that. However, he liked her for whatever reason.

Slipping on a pair of sweat pants, wife beater, and his crispy white One's, he grabbed the milk and headed for the door.

"Missy, I'm takin' yo' hoodrat-ass partner this milk!"

"My friend ain't no hoodrat, boy!"

"Whatever, yo!" BG yelled as he left.

He knocked on the door.

"It's open!"

BG walked in expecting to find Keisha's hungry-ass children sitting at the small dining table, but instead found Keisha standing there in a pair of gray tights that were wedged in between the lips of her fat pussy. *Damn!* BG thought, locking eyes with her monkey.

"Boy, put that milk on the table," Keisha sassed and walked to her bedroom.

BG sat the milk on the table, but he never once took his eyes off of her body. She had a big stupid-ass booty. *Bitch ain't got all them fuckin' kids for nothin'*, BG thought with a smile.

Keisha came back out of her room walking nastier than ever.

"And whatchu smilin' for?" she asked with a seductive smile of her own. The question was purely rhetorical, because she saw exactly where his eyes were roaming and she loved it. She'd always had a thing for BG, and hated that Missy's *goody-two-shoe's* ass had him all to herself. Always bragging about what BG gave her and about how good the dick was. *Hmph*, Keisha thought to herself as she eyed BG, *I know the lil' bougie bitch ain't gon' eat that dick and swallow them nuts like Miss Keisha.*

"Umm, the milk over there," BG said, eyes still fixated on Keisha's goods.

"Boy, you see somethin' you want?"

"What?" BG looked up into her face for the first time. "What happened?"

"Nigga, I seen you." Keisha smiled, rubbing her pussy lips. "Look good, don't it?"

BG didn't know what the fuck to say. He was scared that this whole situation was some kind of test or setup that Missy and Keisha had put together. So he just played stupid like he didn't know what she was talking about. But Keisha was not going for it.

"Boy, I'm not gon' say nothin'."

"Say nothin' 'bout what?"

"'Bout this."

Keisha reached into BG's sweat pants and grabbed his manhood. *Shit!* she thought as she began stroking it hard. It seemed to double in size. *So this bitch wasn't lyin', this dick big as fuck!*

Keisha got down on her knees right there in the living room and sucked her friend's pussy juices off of her man's dick. She could smell the sex in his pubic hairs, but that didn't stop her. It seemed to turn her on even more.

"Mmmm," Keisha moaned as she bobbed her head up and down, taking more and more dick into her mouth with each dip.

"Damn, girl, you're a beast."

BG was loving it. Keisha was a grade-A, certified *head-doctor*. She worked her neck and toyed with his balls like a BadLand Films porn-star. *If the top is Maggie Simpson, I know the bottom is straight Peg Bundy*, BG thought and cupped the back of Keisha's head. He fucked her face like he had fucked Missy that morning. He was about to feed Keisha his unborn kids when a knock sounded from the front door.

"Oh shit!" BG said, slipping his slob-coated penis out of Keisha's head and into his sweats.

"Keisha, BG in there with you?" Missy yelled from the hallway.

¢ ¢ ¢

"We ain't takin' no more shorts!" JackBoy yelled to the crack-head on the other side of the window.

That had to be the tenth crack-head in less than two hours trying to come short with that money. At first he'd simply let it ride, but he couldn't just continue to sit back and let the slick-ass fiends work his little worker, 50. He knew that 50 was new to selling dope and green to all the games that the crack-head veterans played. So he tried to give the young hustler some game.

"50, my nigga, them *custos* gon' keep tryin' you, yo."

"Nah, they straight. He said he gon' bring me the money back."

"And you believe that shit?" JackBoy asked, laughing. "You stupid! Yo' ass better listen to Biggie, *you think a crack-head paying you back, you can forget it!* Straight up."

34

JackBoy really liked 50 because he was a good young dude with plenty of hustle about himself. He just had to learn the tricks of the trade. Once that was done, JackBoy planned to move 50 up the dope-boy corporate ladder, because 50 could be trusted. His money was always on point and JackBoy didn't want to see him serving another nigga's bomb for the rest of his life. He wanted to see 50 with his own shit.

"50, you gotta always remember, *if it don't make dollars, then it don't make sense.* That's the Dade County gospel," JackBoy said.

"I hear you."

"Nah, lil' nigga, do you feel me? 'Cause this shit gon' cost you, yo. Believe that! The game is to be sold, not told."

"Preach, my nigga!" yelled Bo-Jit. "But that young nigga don't want no game, yo."

Bo-Jit was right to a certain extent. 50 was not a real street dude, and selling drugs to helpless addicts was not his favorite activity. 50 just wanted a few dollars in his empty pockets, that way he could live and help his sister with her three children. More so, 50 just wanted to be down. And if that meant selling drugs and soaking up game, then that's what he was going to do. When JackBoy or LG talked, 50 listened as if his life depended on it... because to a degree, it did.

"Man, I'm tellin' you, look at the nigga. He ain't up on game," Bo-Jit ragged 50.

JackBoy looked at 50 and saw that he wasn't going to defend himself. "Nah, don't say that, my lil' nigga's on point."

"You mean yo' lil' son's on point," Bo-Jit snapped. "While you 'round here babyin' niggas, being soft on 50 ain't gon' help 'im in these streets."

Bo-Jit was always hard on 50. Not because he didn't like 50, but because that's how he'd been taught. His whole thing was, you can't be soft on the worker, because if the workers are soft, then the whole squad is soft. Because one day that worker will move up and represent everything that he's been taught.

35

"Bo-Jit, my nigga, you better watch yo' mouth, yo." JackBoy stood up. "I ain't soft on 50 and I don't son no niggas."

"Yeah, well, I can't tell. My nigga, you gotta be hard on these young niggas 'cause these streets ain't gon' take it easy on nobody."

"You right about that," JackBoy had to admit.

JackBoy thought back on the days when he was just a worker. The dude that he worked for was a straight up pimp. JackBoy was new in the streets and the dude took advantage of that. He over worked JackBoy, beat him out of his pay and never played fair with him. But that episode was long over, like water under a bridge. He was still here to play the game—as it should be played—while the fuck-nigga that played him was *out-of-there*, game over for him.

JackBoy believed that what you put into the game was exactly what you got out of the game. That's why he played *all-the-way* fair with the people that he fucked with. 50 was one of those people and he didn't want to see him go through what he'd been through himself.

Bo-Jit's big mouth interrupted his thoughts. "I know I'm right. That nigga Bo-Jit always right, yo!"

"Whatever, nigga." JackBoy brushed him off. "What time did LG say he was comin' through?"

"I don't know, he probably gettin' shit ready for tonight."

"Yeah, that's what he doin'...you right."

"My nigga, that nigga Bo-Jit always right!" Bo-Jit said, laughing at his own arrogance.

¢ ¢ ¢

"Damn!" BG looked around bug-eyed. "Bitch, get yo' ass up and go fix yo' shit!"

BG was stuck like Chuck. He didn't know what to do. One thing was for sure, he was not about to get caught up in no *hoe-shit*.

Keisha wiped her mouth and tried straightening her hair as she ran for her room. She wanted to put on a robe or something more appropriate for the occasion, knowing Missy would snap if she saw her in those painted on tights, in the house with her man.

"Keisha...! BG...! What are y'all doin' in there?" Missy continued to yell.

"Ho-hold up, bay, I'm right here!" BG finally answered.

He took a deep breath and open the door.

"Damn, boy," Missy said.

"What's up, baby?" BG was sweating bullets.

"What are you doin', Keisha done kidnapped you, baby?"

"What?"

"Nothin', boy... where is Keisha?" Missy asked, walking past him.

"She's in the room gettin' the kids outta bed."

"Why're you still here?"

BG thought quick. "Gettin' my milk... shiid, I wasn't 'bout to leave it over here so their asses could drink it up."

The nigga deserved an Oscar. Now his only concern was *could Keisha match his performance.*

"Missy, girl!" Keisha came out in her robe, slippers and scarf. "This crazy nigga of yours act like I won't bring that lil' three dollar ass milk back to y'all."

Missy laughed. "I know his ass is crazy, but I love him."

"Well, you're the only one," Keisha sassed and rolled her eyes.

Missy laughed even harder. "Anyway, y'all, I'm gone. I cannot be late for work."

Missy gave BG a big passionate kiss and left without a clue as to what was going on.

"Damn, you sho' put on good."

37

"Shiid, you too."

Keisha's smile was filled with mischief as she made her way to the window. Watching Missy leave put an even grander stretch of malice across her pretty face. All that she could think of was finishing what she had started. In her twisted mind, she felt that BG somehow cared about her, and that maybe her A-game head would make him leave Missy for her.

"Look, BG."

"What happened, Keisha?"

"Boy, just look."

BG ran over to the window. When he got there Missy's car was just exiting the parking lot. *Fuck did this bitch call me to this damn window for?* he asked himself.

"BeeeeeeeGeeeeeee," Keisha whined from behind him.

He turned to find Keisha's robe at her feet. She was completely naked and looking damn good.

"Girl, are you crazy?"

"No, but you gonna give me some of that dick," Keisha said aggressively.

She pushed BG down on the cool leather couch and quickly snatched his sweats down. A rock hard penis stood facing her.

"Aye, look, Keisha, we don't ne—"

"Boy, shut up!" Keisha straddled him and kissed his lips. "You know you want this."

BG felt the warmth of her womb engulf him. Keisha's pussy was so warm, and so wet... BG grabbed her by the waist and pulled her all the way down, forcing Keisha to take all of him.

"Ooooh, shit!" Keisha yelled. "Boy, wait."

"Nah," he whispered in her ear. "You said you wanted the dick, bitch, now you gon' take all of it."

Keisha began bucking like a wild horse. The dick was killing her. But she loved every minute of it—every inch of it. And wished that somehow he could hurt her more. Keisha was a *stone-cold* pain freak.

"Turn around, turn around... Let me beat this pussy from the back," BG said.

Keisha jumped up and bent over the couch. BG had a good clear view of her fat, hairy pussy. He spread her lips and slammed into her. Keisha gasped, but immediately started throwing it back. Her wide ass jumped and clapped as BG pounded her with no mercy.

"Ooh, BG, I'm cummin'!"

He pounded harder and faster. Her cum covered his dick. She had gotten hers and he was on the verge of getting his. He felt the electrifying feeling build up and before he could explode, BG pulled out and turned Keisha around. She readily accepted him into her mouth, sucking the sperm as fast as it came out.

¢ ¢ ¢

Let's see... what to do today? Fuck that shit, I'm going to get my money... A key of cocaine will get a nigga killed / And a banana-clip will get his whole house flipped... He's bringing danger to the life of his homeboy / You can see the move / but don't let him go alone boy... Bout my money.

The sounds of Trick Daddy bumped as LG made his way to the trap. He was smoking good and feeling *hella* good about himself. He had one of the baddest bitches in the city laying up at his apartment smelling like his dick, and a go-hard twin brother that had a plan to lock down Little Haiti. Yeah, it was going down, because just like Trick Daddy said, "They were 'bout their muthafuckin' money!"

And a new black brome for my new dread home / You ain't been outta jail long / but nigga you dead wrong... 'bout my money, nigga / You shouldn't play wit' it / You gon' remember the day when this AK hitcha...

39

LG hopped out of the car, still smoking big weed, and walked off into the trap-house. He was about his money, which meant that he was ready to count it.

"What's up, yo," JackBoy greeted his man.

"Ain't nothin' ..." LG looked around the spot. "Where's that money?"

50 got up and passed LG the money that he'd made last night. He knew that LG was going to sit there and count *every last dollar.* And then check the dope to make sure he hadn't tapped the sack. It didn't offend 50 because he already knew what it was. It was business. And LG handled his to the fullest.

"It's straight," he finally said.

"So you ready for tonight?" JackBoy asked.

"Shiid, you know it."

The two exchanged dap and LG left to take 50 home.

Chapter 4
It Popped Off

V-Dub sat in his Lexus 430 talking to Nut about the dumb young girls that they'd fucked the previous night. They were parked in Edison Projects waiting on Doc to come out of one of their dope spots. He'd only gone in to pick up some money, but had been gone for damn near thirty minutes.

V-Dub blew the horn. "What the fuck is kid doin' in there?" an upset V-Dub asked.

"Man, I don't know," Nut replied.

"I got shit to do… kid playin' games. He need to hurry his ass up!"

"For real… oh, there he go."

Doc jumped in the car and did not waste anytime telling V-Dub what he'd just heard. Someone had just told him that BG was out of jail and having a big homecoming party tonight.

V-Dub couldn't believe what Doc was saying. He'd been looking for BG for what he'd done to him almost two and a half years ago.

"You sho'?" V-Dub asked.

"That's what Sunny just told me."

V-Dub smiled a wicked smile. "Yeah, aiight then…we goin' to a party tonight, yo."

¢ ¢ ¢

They left the projects and headed straight to V-Dub's crib on 123rd Street and 15th Avenue. The young and up-and-coming niggas called this section of Miami, Westside.

Once inside V-Dub made a few phone calls. He was ready to *get his man*, and needed some AK-47's delivered to him ASAP.

"Yo, Doc, we gon' need a car...nah, better yet, get a van," V-Dub instructed.

"I know who got one," Doc answered, still sitting there.

"Nigga, make it happen!" V-Dub snapped.

Doc got up and flexed back to Little Haiti. He found Sam on 68th, sitting on a milk crate. Sam was the *go-to splackman* whenever anyone in Little Haiti needed a stolen car.

"What it do, yo?" Doc greeted. "I need a auto, yo. A van."

"Aiight, $500, yo."

"I need it by eight o'clock."

"Aiight, yo... eight o'clock," Sam answered, still sitting on his milk crate.

"Nigga, make it happen!" Doc snapped, just like V-Dub had snapped on him.

¢ ¢ ¢

Check it...I'm sick of this bullshit. I want revenge, and umm, I wants the killa... 'Cause I choose when a muthafucka live or die... Payin' my dues fool! I lost a nigga in the struggle / my oldest brutha / but fuck-niggas memories be forever... 'Cause I'ma nigga out the projects see / did time in the joint for muthafucka fuckin' wit' me...Let's get to the bottom of this bullshit / all of a sudden yous a friend of mine / now where you was bitch...

Trick flowed from V-Dub's home entertainment system. He and his right-hand man Nut had already gone and picked up the guns from his uncle's friends, and were now loading and duct-taping the extra clips.

The day had finally arrived and V-Dub didn't plan on squandering the opportunity. He could not wait to hop out unloading the big machine gun that he was now loading.

BG had really tried him. A lot of time had passed since that day, but V-Dub had not forgotten.

"Nut, call Hobba and Von." V-Dub wiped the AK-47 down and placed it on the coffee table. "Tell 'em they ridin', too."

"But we only got four K's."

"Four jumpin' out and somebody gotta drive."

...I'm comin' atcha wit' the thunder and rain / and when I'm squeezin' this thang / yo' attitude gon' change...shootin' AK's / still thankin' 'bout Hollywood / another memory stuck / and it ain't all good. 'Cause he died in his shoes / wit' no clues of the killa / got me screamin'... oh me, oh my, oh Lord...

¢ ¢ ¢

"Man, where the fuck is this *chin-ass* nigga at?" V-Dub asked.

The party was being held on 55th Street and 6th Avenue, so the five heavily armed men sat in the parked van at the corner of 56th Street and 6th. They were waiting for the man of honor. V-Dub couldn't wait to *shower him* with the special gifts that he'd brought him—over 200 rounds of .762's.

From where they sat the goons could see everything that moved on the block. To V-Dub it seemed that every passing minute was an eternity.

"Yo, V, there go lil' bruh right there..." Von said, pointing at LG. "We can hop out and splash his hoe-ass right now."

Nut spoke up. "Nah, we should just wait... get both of them niggas when BG pull up."

Everybody turned to V-Dub, who nodded his approval. Nut was his main man. The two had done so much dirt together that they'd started to think alike.

"Speakin' of the muthafuckin' devil, there he go!" Hobba pointed.

They continued to watch as BG and a *badass* big booty broad got out of the car. They greeted a few people and started making their way towards the door.

"Come on, let's do this!" V-Dub ordered.

Doc, behind the wheel of the stolen mini-van, brought the vehicle to a real slow creep with the lights out.

V-Dub, Nut, Hobba, and Von readied themselves—donning black gloves and ski masks.

The van stopped just as the sliding door opened and all hell broke loose!!!

¢ ¢ ¢

"LG, we're on our way right now," Missy said with a big Kool-Aid smile on her pretty face.

"Aiight then, I'ma have the DJ stop the music."

"Okay, bye."

Missy came back out of the store to find BG blindfolded and looking stupid just like she had left him.

"I don't know how I let yo' crazy-ass talk me into this dumb-ass shit," BG said, not knowing where he was or where he was going.

Missy continued cheesing. "'Cause you love and trust yo' wifey."

That was part of the reason. Yet guilt was the ultimate factor in his decision to let Missy make a fool out of him. He felt terrible about the breach in conduct that he'd committed with Keisha. He had seriously violated, not only his own laws—he vowed to never shit where he ate, which he'd done by fucking his neighbor—but also Missy's love and trust.

"Well," BG finally said. "This surprise better be good, yo."

"Bay, you know yo' wifey get it poppin'," Missy spoke seductively. "So when it pop off, you gonna love it."

BG's mind went straight to the gutter. *Maybe she's gon' ménage the kid trios!* he thought, smiling. *That shit with Keisha might've been a prelude, now they're 'bout to straight run a G on a G.*

That thought kept him smiling all the way to Ms. Gin's house. Ms. Gin was Shara's mother, and for the right fee, she didn't give a damn about them throwing a surprise party for BG at her house. Shit, if they would've upped the ante, she would have jumped out of his cake. Ms. Gin was about her money.

Missy pulled her car up to Ms. Gin's house and hurried around to open BG's door. Just as she opened the door Jay-Z's *Show Me What You Got* exploded from the huge wall of Vegas that took up most of Ms. Gin's living room.

Hearing the loud music, BG quickly snatched off the blindfold. Everybody surrounding the car yelled, *SURPRISE!!!*

BG sat smiling and shaking his head in disbelief. "Aiight, y'all got me... y'all got the kid."

The whole hood was there to show BG some love. They had to, because hands down BG was one of the realist young niggas in the City of Miami. So love it or hate it, bitches and niggas had to respect it.

"Boy, what's up?" Rah-Rah said, hugging his long time partner.

"Shiid, you know how I do."

"Yeah, I know, kid," Rah-Rah replied. "Lil One couldn't make it, yo. He really wanted to fall through, but he in some serious *fuck-shit* wit' that fool Dre and them, he sent this, though."

Rah-Rah passed BG a brick of cocaine. BG smiled and slipped the dope up under the passenger seat. "Man, tell fool, bet that

45

up!" Seeing Keisha, BG made a mental note to fuck Keisha in that big ass of hers the next time.

"Boy, Keisha lettin' these hoes have it, my nigga," JackBoy commented.

"No bullshit. But yo, who's that wit' her?" BG asked.

"Man, that's Mu-Mu, Pinky and Rockel. I don't know who those other two hoes is."

"My nigga, that's Lil Mu-Mu?" BG couldn't believe how fine that little girl had gotten.

"She ain't lil' no more."

"Yeah, you right about that."

People were steady pulling up in all sorts of rides. Some BG knew, but most of them he'd never seen before. He was checking out Lil Mu-Mu and Keisha when he noticed a dark-colored van ease up. He continued to watch as the sliding door flew open, and out jumped his worst nightmare.

Yak! Yak! Yak! Yak! Yak! Yak! sounded one AK-47, followed by *Yyyaaaakkk!!!* Four masked men jumped out cutting loose. Everybody started scattering and hitting the deck.

Boom! Boom! Boom! Boom! LG came up sparking his .40. He continued letting off, but the AK's fire was too heavy. *Boom! Boom! Boom!* he retreated. This was not LG's first gunfight, and he was going to make damn sure that it wasn't his last.

Tat! Tat! Tat! Tat! Tat! JackBoy fired his .9mm, trying to make it to his car where he had a Mini-14 on the backseat.

BG was on the ground as soon as the first round was spent. His new *fit* was fucked up and his mind was racing. *What the fuck is goin' on?* he wondered as he searched for Missy. She was nowhere to be found.

BG pulled his Glock .40 as AK-47 slugs continued to pour through the car that he was hiding under.

Yyyyaaaakkkk!!!! about 60 rounds hit all around him.

BG looked under the car and saw the legs of one of the gun men. He had 31 rounds in his own extended clip, so he promptly

46

sent six in the attacker's direction. *Boom! Boom! Boom! Boom! Boom!*

By now there was complete chaos in the street.

Boom! Boom! Boom! Boom! Boom! Boom! JackBoy was now busting the Mini-14.

He hit one of the masked men it the chest—FLIPPED HIM!!!

Boom! Boom! Boom! Boom! BG kept firing from beneath the car.

The other three masked men felt the heat and turned their attention to BG. *Yak! Yak! Yak! Yak! Yak!*

Boom! Boom! Boom! BG watched as one of the three remaining men dropped.

A fountain of blood poured from the fist-sized hole in his neck.

The tables had turned on the intruders. They fired back and made their way back to the van, leaving their two dead homeboys on the pavement—TWISTED!!!

Once inside, the van sped off.

¢ ¢ ¢

"Yo, LG!" BG screamed for his little brother.

"I'm good, bruh!" LG yelled back from the opposite side of the yard.

Seeing that LG was straight, BG turned his search to Missy. "Missy! Yo, Missy!"

"Over here, BG! Over here!" Shara yelled. "Somebody call 9-1-1, she's been shot!"

BG ran over to Shara, who was kneeling beside Missy. The sight fucked BG up! "Damn, man!" he yelled as he kneeled down beside them, tears were in his eyes.

"Aye, bruh, we gotta go, man," LG whispered to his brother.

"Nah, man."

LG could feel his pain because he loved Shara just as BG loved Missy, and he'd probably be acting the very same way if the bullet were in her. Still, they had to go.

"Look, bruh, the ambulance is comin'... and so is them crackas. We gotta go, kid."

BG's heart screamed, *Fuck you, I'm staying here with Missy because she would stay here with me. She wouldn't be here shot all up if it wasn't for me.* But those were his emotions driving him, while his mind reminded him of Chino's words. "Stay in motion and keep it emotionless."

He definitely had to go. What good would he be to Missy, LG and their squad sitting in prison for murder? How could he avenge this great disrespect if he got jammed-up?

"I gotta go, baby." BG kissed Missy on her forehead. "I love you and I'ma damn sho' ride for you."

He got up and ran off with LG and JackBoy.

¢ ¢ ¢

LG looked at his brother and saw death in his eyes. He really didn't know what to say to him, so he said nothing as the car made its way towards Carol City.

Who the fuck could've done this? LG asked himself. He knew a few niggas that might have had a *slight bit of inside* for their crew, but nothing to this degree.

He needed answers, so he pulled out his cell phone and made a few calls. LG put out the word that he was buying all information concerning the shoot-out, and he was willing to pay top dollar for it. He then hit Shara's phone to see what was up with Missy's condition. He prayed that she was okay.

"Yeah?" Shara answered.

"What's good wit' sis?"

"They got her in the Emergency Room right now... I don't know, bay. Shit lookin' crazy, 'cause ain't nobody tellin' me shit."

"Aiight, I'ma hit you back."

BG didn't bother to ask his brother what was going on with Missy, because if the news was good LG would've just spilled it. He felt bad as he stared out of the window. Seriously wishing that it was him and not her laying in the hospital fighting for dear life... *Damn, why did I fuck Keisha? When for real, all I love is Missy...* Thoughts of marriage and lots of children ran through his confused mind, but he didn't know if that would ever happen.

BG wiped his tear-filled eyes and decided not to punish himself with things that he couldn't control, but instead he'd punish the muthafuckas that violated him with a controlled attack like they'd never witnessed before.

"Yo, call Mono and tell 'im I need some *splacks*," he finally spoke. "Then call Lil One."

"I'm on it, bruh," LG said, dialing the number.

Lil One was Gemo's man, but BG and LG had gotten really close to him. He was a wild young gunslinger that robbed everything outside of his circle.

They didn't hang out at all, but they could always depend on one another for whatever.

Lil One was born and raised in Brown Sub, but could be found hanging anywhere. Nobody really knew where he laid his head.

"Yo, bruh, Lil One said to fall through the Front."

The Front was right off of 191st and 37th Avenue. It was a spot where a gang of drugs were sold. All day long people ran to and from the Front to buy whatever it was that they needed to satisfy their habbits.

When the trio pulled up BG spotted Lil One rapping with their homeboy Var. BG jumped out and walked over. Lil One could see off the rip that something was seriously wrong with his partner. He dapped Var up and walked off with BG.

"What's good, bruh?" Lil One slurred.

BG could see that Lil One was high, the boy was always on pills and lace.

49

"It's all bad, yo," BG said. "Niggas tried to kill me, yo... they hit Missy."

"Yeah, she aiight?"

"I don't know, yo."

Lil One could not believe his ears. He was now as mad as BG, but he maintained his cool and listened. When it was all said and done they agreed to meet up later. Meanwhile, BG and his crew would be lamping at Lil One's honeycomb in Carol City. It was perfect because no one would ever think to look for them out that way.

¢ ¢ ¢

"So what're we gon' do, yo?" JackBoy asked as they headed to the new hideout.

"Fuck you mean, what're we gon' do? Fool, we're gon' war, that's what we're gon' do! My nigga, we gon' kill everybody that I think had somethin' to do wit' this shit," BG fumed.

"That's wit'out sayin', yo. What I'm sayin' though, is we can't trap and war, my nigga."

LG didn't say anything, but he'd been thinking the exact same thing. His mind was in war mode, but he knew that it took finances to fund a war. Finances that they really didn't have. After all, their money came from their one trap, and if whoever pulled that *fuck-shit* at the party knew enough to know about the party, they sure as hell knew about the trap.

"JackBoy's right, bruh," LG spoke up. "Beef is beef, fuck it, we'll kill 'em all. A nigga done been there and done that... for real, them *chin-ass* niggas ain't ready for the drama we bringin'. But, bruh, we gon' need money. Straight up!"

BG had come home prepared to make a real power move. But now look. Shit was all fucked up, and getting worse by the minute.

"Look, I feel y'all boys. So we're gon' let yo' lil' man, 50, run the spot while we bury these niggas... shit's simple."

"Yeah, that'll work," JackBoy said.

With that shit out of the way LG could concentrate on what he was best at, *fucking niggas over.* The suckers had made the first move, but LG was preparing to make the best move...

Chapter 5
Everything's In Order

Early the next morning the shooting was all over the news and in the newspapers. BG knew that it would be, with two men dead and a woman in critical condition, it would be like *First 48.* As he sat smoking 'dro and watching Channel 7 WVSN's report of the killing, he couldn't help but to relive the events in his mind. *I should have made sure that Missy was straight... I shouldn't have ever fucked Keisha... It should be me in the hospital and not Missy... Damn! Who the fuck could've done this shit?* BG thought to himself. On the scene a reporter was now interviewing the lead Detective on the case.

"Well what can you tell us so far, Detective?"

"Right now, details are very sketchy. What we do know is that the young lady in the coma, suffering from a gunshot wound to the head, has a boyfriend that may somehow be linked to this ugly situation."

"Is he a suspect in the shooting?"

"No, he's not, but we have reason to believe that he was the intended target."

"Why do you believe so?"

"I'm sorry, but I am not at liberty to disclose that information."

"Do you have the names of the two men that were killed or the young lady who's fighting for her life?"

"Yes, we have identified the men and the young woman, but we are holding this information until the families have been notified."

"Thank you, Detective... This is Greg Veludez with Channel 7 Eye Witness News, now back to you, Bob."

After hearing the news cast BG was really fucked up. To hear that Missy was in a coma brought tears to his eyes. He wanted so badly to see her, however he also knew that the hospital was off-limits to him. The police would be laying for him to do something as stupid as trying to visit Missy. He had no intentions of talking to the police about anything. He wondered if anyone had mentioned to the police that he had a gun that night, or worse, that he'd killed one of the masked shooters.

Things were not looking good for him at all. His girl was in danger of losing her life, police were looking for him, and somebody wanted him dead. "Fuck this shit!" BG said out loud. Nothing was going to stop him from finding and killing the other dudes in that van. BG was prepared to beat the streets for everything they had to offer, and punish them for every infraction that he'd suffered because of them. Somebody knew something, and it was only a matter of time before he found out.

"What's up, bruh?" LG greeted his big brother.

He'd just entered the living room and found BG's eyes glued to the TV screen.

"Ain't shit, bruh," BG responded, passing LG the remains of his blunt. "You aiight?"

"Yeah, I'm good." LG hit the weed. "You look like you ain't get much sleep last night."

BG thought for a moment. "I didn't, but I'ma make damn sure that the fuck-nigga behind this bullshit gon' get a gang of sleep... In the comfort of a casket."

¢ ¢ ¢

V-Dub was extremely upset that Von and Hobba had both gotten slumped last night. But what really pissed him off was the fact that BG and LG were still breathing. Not only had he lost two good men, but there now lay a great propensity of *all-out-war*. Something that he didn't want or need.

"Yo, V! I heard BG's bitch got hit last night, yo," Doc said.

"Who told you that?"

"The nigga Sunny, who else?"

Now shit was really heating up. He knew that BG and his squad would be out beating the block for information, and when they struck pay dirt, *all-out-war* was imminent.

"Yo, I need you and Nut to hit the street. See if niggas know anything, you feel me? We gotta stay at least two steps ahead of them *chin-ass* niggas." V-Dub spoke with plenty of confidence and a cool smirk on his face, but inside his stomach was sour, because he could already feel the pressure.

As soon as Nut and Doc were gone, V-Dub left to go talk to his uncle. His uncle was a smart, laid-back businessman, and drugs just so happened to be his business.

V-Dub never let his uncle know about what he was personally doing in the streets—as far as the beefing and the dumb shit. Because he knew that his uncle would cut him off.

He often schooled V-Dub on the aspects of surviving the dope-game. Number one was to *play fair with those that played fair*... Number two was to *stay low and humble*...Number three was *always save for a rainy month*, because the span of a day wasn't enough...Fourth was to *keep wars to a minimum*. Violence should always be a last recourse... And lastly, *see all endeavors through to the end*...

Of course V-Dub didn't hear any of that shit. V-Dub wanted the spotlight and recognition more than he wanted the money.

Nut and Doc hit the block wide open. But they weren't asking any questions about the shooting, they were busy asking bitches for some quick *action*. "Why ride 'round on some *detective-ass-shit* when we can be *shonin'*, yo?" Doc had said, hitting the blunt. Nut laughed with his man, but replied sternly, "Yeah, I feel you, yo... but yo' man Sunny better have the 4-1-1, or V-Dub gon' kill me... then, I'ma kill you."

The two continued riding around until they came up on two *live-wire-shones* cruising Bayside. With little or no game, the promise of some pills and a good time, they were off to the hotel. But before any games could begin, Nut had to cover his ass.

"Doc, call that nigga Sunny back and see what it do."

"Damn, Nut, ain't no pressure, yo... we gon' handle that, chill." Doc played it, trying to make it to his room where his *action* was already naked and on two pills.

"Nigga, it is pressure!" Nut snapped. "Now get that nigga back on the phone!"

Fortunately for Doc, Sunny answered on the third ring.

"What it do, yo?"

"You heard anything 'bout what I asked you earlier?"

"Yeah, I heard somethin'."

"What?" Doc asked impatiently. He loved the information, but hated the source, because Sunny was a scared-ass bitch that talked too much.

"Man, some niggas shot up kid's party last night, but don't nobody know who. They say kid scared as fuck though, and him and LG flexed up outta town."

"Oh yeah? Where you hear that?"

"Look, yo, that's the word. The streets got a lotta eyes and ain't none of 'em seen them niggas."

"Yeah, aiight, bet that up, Sunny. Keep your eyes and ears open, and keep me informed. I gotchu, yo."

"Yeah aiight, I gotcha."

Doc ran down the info to Nut and ran off to join his primary action.

¢ ¢ ¢

"LG, what we did offa that comin' home present that Lil One shot a nigga?"

"Shiid, 'bout 21,000, but we still gotta nine-piece left offa it, and we ain't paid the workers."

BG thought for a minute. "Well pay 'em, and then get all that bread up. I'm 'bout to hit the new connect and see what's up."

Once everything was in proper order with the work and the trap, BG planned to run up the murder per capita in the GunShine State.

He instructed LG to holla at Shara and her sisters—Nesha and Tasnim—because they were going to need some rental cars to move around in. LG's Max was too flashy and everybody knew the car. With fresh tinted-out rentals they could move undetected. They would also need some big guns and plenty of rounds.

¢ ¢ ¢

ZoeMan's favorite place to eat, besides his wife's kitchen, was a Haitian eatery on 54th Street and 2nd Avenue called Chef Creole's. He ate there all of the time, therefore he was very popular amongst the people that ate and worked there.

BG agreed to meet ZoeMan there at three o'clock sharp. ZoeMan hated people that wore sagging pants, people that sported gold-teeth and most of all, people that did lazy business. So BG made sure he was fresh and neatly dressed and most of all, on time.

BG had been introduced to ZoeMan—who controlled about 65% of the cocaine in Miami—through his big cousin Gemo. When

Gemo caught his federal time he passed most of his useful connects to his little cousin, BG.

As BG sat in his ride, in the restaurant's parking lot, waiting for ZoeMan to arrive, he thought about Missy. He'd talked to Missy's cousin, Muffin, earlier and nothing had changed. She was still in ICU barely holding on. The doctors said that Missy had lost a tremendous amount of blood and things just did not look good.

BG closed his woeful eyes for a moment to pray on Missy's behalf. He prayed that God would allow her to pull through and once again be a part of his life. BG promised that this time he would love her the way that she was supposed to be loved.

When he opened his eyes again he peeped a black BMW 750Li pulling up. He wondered if it was ZoeMan. His question was answered when his cell phone began ringing.

"I hope you are here," ZoeMan said simply.

"Yeah, I'm here, in the white Dodge Charger."

"Come, let's talk money."

BG got out of his rental and climbed into the backseat of ZoeMan's plush luxury vehicle. There was another Haitian man in the car with ZoeMan—his right-hand man, Frantz.

The three greeted one another and got down to business. ZoeMan could get BG anything he wanted and guarantee that it would always be at least 85% pure. So BG could just about do anything he wanted with the cocaine and still have fire product.

The terms were BG was to deal with Frantz and Frantz alone. He would be fronted whatever he purchased and expected to pay $15,000 (which was a godfather deal) per brick. The balance would be due five days from the time he received the work, and the very first time that he was late or short would be his last.

"You understand?" ZoeMan asked, staring BG in the eyes.

"Yeah, I gotchu."

"Please stay low-key, play fair, save your money, no violence if it's not necessary, and always see things through... You will go far, like Gemo."

"Okay."

"Good, Frantz will see you tonight." ZoeMan never smiled during the entire course of their conversation. "Everything's in order."

¢ ¢ ¢

Meanwhile JackBoy and Bo-Jit were over at the new trap-house on 55th Street and 5th Avenue getting things in order. They had a crack-head to put in a new AC unit, and clean up the house. JackBoy was working overtime trying to get all of the new spots up and running. BG had already secured the connect, 50 and Teddy P had been schooled on the responsibilities of being lieutenants, and now it was time for retaliation.

When JackBoy and Bo-Jit were finished, they paid Pop the crack-head and were about to leave when Sunny pulled up.

"Yo, JB, check this out, yo!"

JackBoy couldn't imagine what Sunny might want, because for real – for real, he didn't really rock with Sunny like that.

"What's up, yo?" JackBoy asked when he reached the car.

"Man, I know who shot BG's ho—, I mean girl."

"Nigga, what?"

"I know who shot her, yo," Sunny repeated.

"Who?"

"Them niggas Doc, Nut, and V-Dub had somethin' to do wit' it, yo."

JackBoy knew exactly who the three niggas were, and knew for certain why they'd done it. BG and V-Dub used to do business a few years back, but some crazy shit had taken place and BG fucked V-Dub over.

"How the fuck you know?"

"The nigga Doc been callin', sweatin' me 'bout info, asking have I heard anything 'bout who done it, or whatever."

58

JackBoy reached into his pocket and gave Sunny a grand. "Bet that up, kid... I 'preciate the info." JackBoy's mug was bent. "I really do."

Sunny peeped JackBoy's murderous expression. "Well, you ain't heard that shit from me." With that said, and money in hand, he sped off.

¢ ¢ ¢

V-Dub was at home enjoying Trina's tight, succulent pussy. He had her in the buck giving her straight pound game. V-Dub stabbed and beat as if there were no tomorrow and Trina couldn't get enough.

She was not the type of chick that wanted to be romanced, Trina wanted to be fucked, used and abused. If she didn't cum in every position—doggie style, froggy style, the buck, spoon, cowgirl, and in the ass—she would throw a complete tantrum— usually tearing up V-Dub's house and fucking up his car.

She was a crazy, *freak-bitch*, but V-Dub absolutely loved her. He'd met her at a BadLand's release party. She was doing porn at the time. After one night of sex with her, V-Dub decided to suit up—cape, tights, knee-high boots and all, and save her.

"Whose pussy is this?"

"It's yours, daddy! Now get it, get it, daddy," the 5'7", 140 pound, dime piece yelled.

Porn-star, gold-digger, shone, pill-animal...V-Dub didn't care because he loved her. Sucker, Captain-save-a-hoe, trick-ass nigga, pussy whipped... Call it whatever, it didn't matter because he loved her...

After Trina finally decided she'd had enough, she and V-Dub hit the shower and got fresh to death. She had appointments at both the hair and nail salon, which cost V-Dub $750, and he had to meet up with Nut to handle some business.

¢ ¢ ¢

V-Dub cruised along listening to Drake's *Best I Ever Had* and couldn't help but think of Trina. She was his one sure weakness; he'd do anything for her.

When he made it to the stash-house in *Robbin Hood*, on 88th Street and 16th Avenue, Nut was already there waiting in his car.

"You late, nigga!" Nut spat with attitude.

"Man, Trina had a nigga tied up."

"Yeah, I bet."

The stash-house only had a TV and a bed. No one lived there. The sole purpose of the house was to stash and bag up drugs. From time to time Nut would bring one of his stripper hoes over and freak off. Of course, V-Dub knew nothing about Nut using the stash-house as a motel.

"Get that work outta the back room," V-Dub instructed as he set up the table.

Nut came back shortly after. "V, it's only two bricks left, yo."

"Yeah, I know, I sold a nigga four."

The two men went to work. Nut—the Whip King of Lil Haiti—whipped up one of the bricks while V-Dub sacked up the other one in *raw twenties* and *dimes*. V-Dub never cut his cocaine, that's why his spots stayed leaping. Netting him about $30,000 off of each kilo.

"Aye, Nut, I'ma need some more 34-34's."

"We gon' have to get some, it's only 12-12's left in here."

"Fuck it, I'll help you bust-down the hard and I'll finish this later."

The two men would be there for the rest of the night cutting up crack and talking about putting an end to the growing situation with BG and his crew.

Chapter 6
Let the Games Begin

LG got to the hideout in Carol City that Lil One had let them hole up in. He got there before BG. Only JackBoy and Bo-Jit were inside. Over two blunts of 'dro, JackBoy told LG everything that Sunny had told him. LG hit the roof.

"Man, I told that nigga to off kid!" LG yelled.

LG was ready to kill V-Dub. The worst part was that the nigga should have been dead. He'd begged BG to let him kill V-Dub, but BG wouldn't give him the green light. Now look, LG always knew that what they'd done to V-Dub would come back to haunt them.

LG also knew exactly where he could find them, Edison Projects. Getting in and out of those projects wasn't going to be an easy task, because Edison Projects were made sort of like a maze. V-Dub had surely picked a fine spot to hole up.

"How we gon' handle this, yo?" Bo-Jit asked.

"We gon' kill them fuck-niggas, that's how!" LG yelled in response.

BG walked in on the tail end of his brother's statement. "What's up, bruh?"

"That nigga V-Dub and them *booty-ass* niggas he be wit' shot up the fuckin' party!"

As soon as BG heard the name V-Dub, he thought back to what LG had told him all those years ago. "Don't let that nigga live, bruh... I'm tellin' you!"

"How y'all know all this?" BG asked.

"Sunny told me. He said the niggas called him asking funny-ass questions about the shit that happened, on some *who-knew-what* type shit," JackBoy told his man.

"Them niggas tryna find out if we know yet," Bo-Jit stated.

"Yeah..."

"Well, look, I gotta plan."

BG let everyone know, then and there, what he needed them to do. He had to meet Frantz later to pick up the dope. LG and Bo-Jit were to take one of the rentals and do their homework on V-Dub's operation. They needed to know who worked there and when or/if V-Dub ever showed his face at the spot. They also needed to send someone up in the spot to cop.

"We should send a hoe," JackBoy suggested.

"Why?"

"'Cause most likely one of the fuck-niggas gonna try and holla, and if they do, we in," JackBoy explained.

"Yeah, he right. So getta hoe," BG said.

"I gotta hoe, too, she's perfect," LG stated.

"Okay, JackBoy, holla at Mono 'em. We gon' need some cars. Make sure them shits is fast, 'cause we 'bout to hit them niggas hard!"

"I'm on it, BG."

BG was now back in the driver's seat, because the element of surprise was back on his side. V-Dub and his crew had no idea that BG was aware of his attempt on his life. So he couldn't possibly know that BG was coming with murderous intent.

¢ ¢ ¢

62

The bitch that LG had in mind was perfect for the job. She was a stripper that went by the name Black Barbie, standing 5'8", 135 pounds, with long silky black hair and skin as dark as a moonless night. Barbie was a bad bitch. There was nothing average about her 38-24-40. LG kept her number just for times like this.

"Hello."

"What's up, Black Girl?"

"Who the fuck is this?"

"This LG, Gemo's lil' cousin."

"Oh, what's up, boo?"

"Money, that's what's up."

LG explained everything in detail that he needed her to do. He left out all of the shit concerning the beef, but promised her 65% of everything that the robbery netted.

"Sixty-five?" she questioned.

"Yeah, sixty-five."

"When?" Was the money hungry bitch's next question.

"ASAP!"

"I'll see you first thang tomorrow, baby."

¢ ¢ ¢

BG got the call from Frantz about 9:30 p.m. They agreed to meet in the parking lot of Club Lexx, on 27th Avenue and 120th Street. The location was perfect because it was on front street, and lots of flashy cars came in and out of the parking lot. So if the *crackas* were watching, they wouldn't be paying attention to the undercover that BG was riding in.

"BG, where are you?" Frantz asked as he pulled into the parking lot.

"I'm in the black G-6."

"I see you."

Frantz parked two cars down and signaled for BG to walk down to the silver Range Rover. Once BG was inside Frantz passed him a bag with five kilos inside. BG checked the work and then handed Frantz a bag containing $35,000.

"Everything's straight, BG?"

"Yeah, that's 35,000, so we're at 40,000 now."

"See you in five days."

BG got out of the Rover and quickly hopped back into the speedy Pontiac G-6. He fired up the engine and started out of the parking lot. He came down 121st Street and turned right on Gulf Drive. But so did a white Ford LTD with *dark-boys* on it. BG watched in his rearview mirror as the car followed him onto 119th Street, travelling east. Once he crossed 10th Avenue and saw that he'd easily made the 7th Avenue light to access the I-95 South on ramp, he picked up his cell phone and hit speed dial.

"What's good?" Lil One answered.

"Everythang's everythang, you can turn off. I got it from here."

"Aiight, fool, holla later," Lil One capped and turned the white LTD right on 7th Avenue, headed to the after-hour.

BG didn't trust anyone outside of his unit, not even ZoeMan. He had Lil One posted up in the Lexx parking lot, *just in case.* Now that the deal was over and he was stash-house bound, he called LG to let him know that everything was in order.

¢ ¢ ¢

The next day LG and Black Barbie met for lunch. He couldn't believe how *bad* Barbie was. He'd seen her before, yet it seemed that she'd gotten finer and prettier since the last time they'd hooked up.

After eating he explained things again. Then he drove her through Edison Projects and pointed out V-Dub's trap. Everything seemed fairly simple to her, so she wanted to get right to work.

LG dropped her off to her car and she doubled back. Always dressed to kill, she jumped out in some tight white Capri shorts, six-inch heels, and a sheer pink button-down shirt. Beneath it she worked a fancy laced bra, cleavage was on full display.

Spotting Doc, Barbie ran her hand through her long black hair, smiled seductively, and *top-modeled* her way over to where he was standing. With all of the *sas* that she put into her *shay*, she could've easily mesmerized any man, woman or child, and left the most venomous King Cobra fangless and spellbound. Poor Doc didn't stand a chance as he stood there wide-eyed and drooling.

"Boy, where can I buy some weed from 'round here?" she asked with her finger in her mouth.

"Umm, shiid, you ain't gotta buy no weed, baby. I gotchu," Doc tried to cap.

"Boy, puleez, I–am–not–your–baby."

"Not yet, but what's yo' name?"

Doc couldn't believe how *bad* the bitch was. His eyes constantly shifted from Barbie's fat pussy print to her firm *she-melons*, to her gorgeous face and back down. Baby was a dime ten times over, and he had to have her.

"I'm not hardly tellin' yo' butt my name," Black Barbie said, rolling both her neck and eyes as she spoke, slightly smiling at the same time. The mixed messages that she sent desiccated what was left of Doc's defenses and common fucking sense. "Y'all niggas in Dade County are some fools, not!"

"Nah, baby, I'm good people. This is my trap right here," Doc lied. "You can't lose wit' Doc, I'm like Allstate, you're in good hands fuckin' wit' me."

Doc was on his *boss-man* shit. Trying like hell to impress the baddest bitch he'd ever seen in his life. She just stood there smiling. Then turned to look around at her surroundings, but more so to give Doc a clear shot of her fat, perfectly round ass.

Facing him again she continued, smiling. "Good hands, huh?"

Doc must've never heard that hit single *Poison* by BBD, because at that instance he'd fallen helplessly for the *big butt and a smile.*

"Look, baby, it's whatever. I mean, I got it." Doc flashed a big wad of V-Dub's money and capped on. "I'm just tryna see you straight and have some fun at the same time... We can hang out, do whatever, 'cause I got plenty money."

"Where we goin', boy?" Black Barbie asked in her little girl's voice, all the while slipping two *honeybees* and three fifties off of Doc's roll.

"Shiid, wherever you wanna go," Doc said quickly and hurriedly put the money back into his pocket. He only made $175 a day and she'd just finessed him for $350. V-Dub was going to kill him. But fuck it, he'd die happy if he could fuck Black Barbie first.

"Okay, give me your number." Black Barbie programmed Doc's phone number in her phone. "That's Tamika, boy..." she flirted extra hard. "I'ma call you later, *Mr. Allstate.*"

Doc's dick damn near jumped out of his shorts, watching her chunk ass and rock her hips as she strolled off. He knew that any bitch that walked that nasty had to be a low-down, filthy bitch in the bed, and he could not wait to find out.

¢ ¢ ¢

As soon as she made it to her car Black Barbie called LG. She gave him the whole rundown on who she'd met and how many dudes she saw working in the trap.

"That was child's play, baby." Black Barbie laughed. "Fool s'posed to get up with me tonight or whatever... thank he 'bout to get some, but not! I'll let you know what's up, though."

"Good, I'ma snatch the nigga tonight."

"Whatever, LG, just have me, me...I don't want no bullshit, 'cause I did what you asked—"

"Barbie, Barbie, slow down. A nigga gotchu. You're Gemo's people, so I would never play no games witchu."

"Yeah, aiight, nigga," Barbie said with a little laugh.

66

With everything officially in order, LG told Barbie what to do next. She was to have Doc meet her in the Grave Yard Projects on 71st Street and NE 2nd Avenue. It was the perfect spot for an ambush because there was only one way in and one way out.

"I'll call you as soon as everything is straight," she said and hung up before LG could say anything further.

¢ ¢ ¢

JackBoy was in one of the stolen cars that he'd bought from Mono with 50 following close behind him so that the police couldn't slide in behind him. JackBoy planned to stash the cars in Edison Towers, he chose this location because the police rarely went through there and it wasn't too far from the hit's destination.

JackBoy parked the first car and jumped in with 50. They had three more cars to move. Then he would drop 50 off at the spot to help Teddy P sack-up the work for the traps.

When they pulled back up to Mono's crib there were more dudes there from Mono's car stealing ring. Rah-Rah, Pachy, Steve, Sam and RayBay were all on the porch smoking weed.

"What's up, y'all boys?"

"You know how we do, JackBoy... just chillin'," RayBay replied.

"Whatchu doin' out here, kid? Ain't y'all boys beefin'?" Steve asked. He'd heard all about what was going on because the streets talked.

"I'm good, yo. Fuck them E.P. *chins*!" JackBoy said with conviction.

"Just be on point, kid."

"I stay on point and I stay strapped."

With that clear JackBoy jumped in another stolen car and took off with 50 right behind him.

¢ ¢ ¢

LG met up with his brother to let him know that the baby was in and the ambush was on. But BG wasn't feeling the setup and snatch. He wanted to lock and unload. BG wanted somebody dead. Not only for Missy being shot, but for the outright disrespect. Gemo was a made man, and he was BG's cousin, so that made BG untouchable. The attack on his party, in his own hood, was a serious blow to BG's reputation. Something that he'd spent long hours in the trenches, countless encounters with death, and many days in confinement to build. The name itself— Big Gangsta—was not only his persona, it was his life. His cornerstone of power. So if he allowed it to slip he would be leaving himself vulnerable to further disrespect, and more open attacks on his established dominion.

"Get Black Girl on the phone," BG ordered.

LG connected the lines. "Hello," Black Barbie answered.

"We gotta problem, Black... We can't wait 'til tonight, we gotta snatch kid now."

"Who the fuck is this?" Black Barbie questioned.

"BG!"

"Oh, well, y'all got too much goin' on for me. I told yo' bro—"

"Look, Barbie, just call the nigga and see where he's at and what he on. We'll do the rest," BG stated.

"And my money?" she needed to know.

"Barbie, we gotchu, I promise."

"Yeah, aiight... y'all hold on... Matter of fact, I'ma call y'all back in ten minutes."

Black Barbie hung up again before a response was given.

BG and LG got *blacked out* and *strapped up*.

"Call JackBoy and tell him we need a *splack*."

LG got on the phone. "Yo, where you at...? Oh yeah...? Well we need one now... Okay, in the park on 53rd Street in five minutes."

¢ ¢ ¢

When the two brothers pulled up at the park JackBoy was leaning against a dark-blue Nissan Pathfinder with his trusty Mini-14 in hand. BG got out with his AR-15, followed by LG with a fully-automatic MAC-90. They exchanged greetings with JackBoy and jumped in the truck, destination Edison Projects.

As they hit 54th Street, LG's cell phone went off. It was Black Barbie.

"Yeah?" LG answered.

"He there."

"You sure?"

"I just talked to the nigga."

"How long ago?"

"When we hung up, nigga!" Barbie yelled, obviously sick of LG, BG and this whole bullshit.

"Look, Barbie, call the nigga back on the three-way and keep 'im on the phone."

"For what?"

"'Cause I need you to! This shit is serious, bit—, I mean, girl... You want yo' money, right?"

Barbie sighed heavily. "Yeah, aiight... But y'all niggas can lose my number after this shit, 'cause y'all got too much shit with y'all! And I swear, y'all better have my muthafuckin' money to-night!"

Barbie clicked over and called Doc back. He answered on the fourth ring, however he was no longer at the spot. Doc foolishly told Black Barbie that he was up at Midway—a corner store on 64th Street and 2nd Avenue. LG quickly whispered the information to JackBoy. They were already on 62nd and 2nd, so Doc was literally seconds away from death.

Black Barbie kept him on the phone, talking as if she was going to truly rock his world tonight.

"There he go right there!" JackBoy pointed as Doc came out of the store with his cell phone to his ear, and a bag in his other hand.

Doc never saw the hit coming.

When JackBoy whipped up into the small parking lot, LG was already out of the car.

Boom! Boom! Boom! Boom! the AR-15 sounded. *Yyyyaaaaaakkkk!* the Mac-90 called out. The only thing louder than the sounds of the guns were Black Barbie's screams through the phone.

Both brothers were unloading before the Pathfinder had come to a complete stop.

Doc dropped his cell phone and reached for his Glock .40, but it was hopeless. The rounds from the two deadly assault rifles tore through his body like paper in a shredder.

Blood covered the parking lot's asphalt. Doc was dead, yet shots continued. BG stood over Doc's lifeless body and emptied the remainder of his 30 round clip.

Boom! Boom! Boom! Boom! Boom! Boom! All face and chest shots.

"Come on, y'all!" JackBoy yelled from inside the truck.

The two gunmen jumped back in and JackBoy sped off into traffic...

¢ ¢ ¢

Nut had been out all night *shoning* with two *pill-animals* that he'd picked up in Club Bed. He was tired as hell and needed to blow one before he started fucking with that trap shit. At times it seemed that he had no life outside of the trap. If he wasn't in the trap, he was sacking up work for the trap, or out gunning at a nigga behind some shit concerning the trap... The trap was just what it was, a muthafucking TRAP!

Nut already had the *pine and dust* mixed in a twenty dollar bill, but as he pulled up to the trap-house in Edison Projects, he realized he was out of Dutch's. *Damn!* he thought and pulled off heading to the corner store.

70

In the distance Nut heard a rapid session of *gunfire* erupt. He didn't think much of it, because guns were always blowing in Little Haiti.

He picked up his cell phone to check on Doc. The nigga was supposed to have been in the trap, but his car wasn't there when he'd just passed.

"Voice mail," Nut said to himself. "I wonder where this freak-ass nigga at?"

As Nut drove down 2nd Avenue, heading to Midway, he peeped a blue Pathfinder hauling ass up out of the parking lot. Then he noticed something that fucked up his entire world. Doc's dead body was swimming in a pool of his own blood, right beside his car.

He could not stand to look at his little man like that, so he continued on past the store. He immediately called V-Dub.

"What it do, kid?" V-Dub answered.

"Doc's dead," Nut whispered into the phone.

"What!" V-Dub screamed.

Nut could only tell him what he knew and that was, *Doc's dead.* He explained what he'd seen, but he didn't say what he felt. Which was, *BG had retaliated.* Of course, he could tell that V-Dub was thinking the same thing, because he heard the tremble in his voice.

"Shut the traps down 'til we handle this," V-Dub ordered.

"'Til we handle what?"

"This shit wit' Doc's murder!" V-Dub yelled.

"Aiight, but who gon' tell kid's old-girl?"

"Shiid, let the police do their job," V-Dub said and hung up.

¢ ¢ ¢

Nut picked up a bottle of Jack Daniels from The Tree and just rode. He sure was going to miss Doc. The younger dude was somewhat of a *fuck up*, but he was also a good, loyal dude. Nut

71

thought about the shit that V-Dub had said concerning telling Doc's momma about what happened to her youngest son. Yeah, the police would inform the family, but *why should they have to when Doc was their friend?* Nut thought as he reentered the hood. He made up his mind that he would drop by Doc's mother's house and pay his respects. *Fuck what V-Dub was talking about.* But first he had to see Sunny. Sunny always seemed to know something about something.

Nut took a big gulp of the strong whisky and leaned hard into the custom leather interior of his Cadillac. Looking through blood-shot eyes, he saw Sunny coming out of BAWA—a corner store on 54th Street and 5th Avenue.

Nut blew his horn to get Sunny's attention. "Yo, Sunny, check this out."

Sunny quickly ran over and got in the car. Nut didn't waste anytime asking Sunny about what he knew, but this time Sunny was truly clueless. Of course, he wasn't going to tell Nut that he was the dirty underhanded muthafucka that put BG and his squad on to them.

"Nah, yo, I ain't know nothin' 'bout that. Damn, that's fucked up that kid got caught up like that," Sunny said, sadly shaking his head.

"Well, have you been seein' them niggas BG and 'em?"

"Nah, but them niggas gotta trap right there."

"Where?"

"Right there," Sunny said, pointing at the house they had on 55th Street. Sunny was *dead-ass-wrong*. He was playing both sides from the middle, which was a very dangerous game.

He didn't care who won the war, he only cared about what he got paid and the winner being in debt to him for his information.

"Who all be there, yo?"

"Some lil' niggas. I hardly ever see them slide through," Sunny answered.

Nut told Sunny to call him the next time that he saw 50 or any of the niggas at the trap. Sunny agreed. Nut shot him half a stack and left for Doc's mother's house.

¢ ¢ ¢

"Just go park that shit in 37th Avenue apartments. I'll be right behind you," BG told JackBoy and followed him to dump the Pathfinder that they'd slumped Doc in.

LG stayed at the hideout with Lil One and told him how they'd caught the fool Doc slipping. Lil One wished like hell he could've been there.

"The bitch-ass nigga looked like he saw a fuckin' ghost," LG explained.

"Yeah, I bet he did," Lil One coldly replied.

Lil One was about six years older than BG, LG and their little squad; so he'd been there and done a whole lot of that. Still, he could really appreciate seeing a hoe-ass nigga get his whole shit tore off.

"You wanna pill, *yo-boy?*"

"Hell nah, nigga! Straight 'dro over here," LG said, pulling out an ounce.

The two partners fell back and did them to the new *One Love* DVD.

¢ ¢ ¢

As BG and JackBoy made their way back to Lil One's hideout, his cell phone rang. It was Keisha. *Damn, maybe Missy done woke up outta her coma,* he thought as he picked up the phone.

"What's up, *yo-girl?*"

"Hey, BG, how you been?"

"I'm good. You been by the hospital to check on Missy?"

73

"Yeah, ain't nothin' changed," Keisha said. "It was some detective that came by her room talkin' wit' her momma."

"Them crackas ain't got no name for me, right?" BG was a little worried at the mention of the detective.

"Not from what I know," Keisha lied.

The confused bitch had the detective on the line as she spoke with BG. He wanted her to keep BG on the line long enough to trace his phone. They'd been looking high and low for the *missing boyfriend* that had been on the scene of the party shooting.

The police had come to Keisha's apartment early that morning after the shooting. She was smoking weed and helping her children get ready for school. The detectives went into their good cop, bad cop bullshit, threatening to have Child Services take her children, and lock her up for a variety of fallacious charges. Aiding and abetting a fugitive, obstruction of justice, principle to murder, possession of drugs, disorderly household, child neglect and contributing to the delinquency of a minor. Truthfully, Keisha could never, in any court of law, be convicted of any of the said charges. But like most black people she was ignorant to the law and easily tricked into cooperating. In her ignorance, Keisha placed BG on the scene of the shooting and stated that she'd seen him shooting at the masked men.

"Look, when Missy wake up outta that coma, I need for you to tell her why I wasn't there with her. You hear me Keisha?" BG asked sadly.

"You know I gotchu, BG... but, umm, can we meet up later and talk right quick?"

BG really didn't mind meeting her, but he really had shit to do.

"Not right now, Keisha."

"Then, when?" Keisha whined.

A few thoughts ran through BG's mind, the main one being, *I know this bitch ain't tryna fuck a nigga after what happened to Missy... 'specially while she in a fuckin' coma.*

74

"Yo, look, I'ma holla later and let you know somethin', but I gotta go now," BG said slowly and hung up before Keisha could speak another word.

¢ ¢ ¢

"We got 'im! He's in the Miami Gardens area," yelled Detective Sims.

"Can I please go now?" Keisha begged. She hated herself for the shit that she'd just done to BG.

Detective Sims frowned on Keisha and pointed his finger in her scared face as he spoke. "You look here, young lady, and you listen good. You are still in a helluva lot of trouble until we catch this guy. So don't get sassy! Do you understand?"

Keisha nodded her head up and down. There were tears in her sad, frightened eyes. She was so afraid of losing her freedom and her children.

"Ms. Jones, if he calls you again, you set a meeting and contact me or my partner immediately. Do you understand?" Sims' partner, Detective Williams, instructed Keisha.

"Yes, sir."

"You are free to go... for now."

Keisha's *not so sweet* life had gotten all the more bitter in a matter of days. First she'd fucked her good friend's man, and now she was helping the police to arrest the same man.

She thought as she rode. Getting past all of this was what she had to do. Keisha pulled into the Quick Stop to get a four pack of Jack Daniels wine coolers, a box of Backwoods Sweet, and some gas.

After paying for her items, she headed for the door. As she exited the store someone called out something to her. When she turned around to see who it was, she couldn't identify the person.

"I'm sorry, but do I know you?" she asked the man that stood before her.

"Nah, lil' momma, not for real." The dude smiled. "But at the same time, I'm really tryna change that."

Keisha looked him up and down and kind of liked what she saw. He was tall, dark and all too handsome. It was obvious that he worked out, his shirt hugged his muscular upper body. *Nice,* Keisha thought.

She smiled at him and walked out of the store. There were things in her life that she needed to be resolved, and *adding a fine-ass-thug* to the equation probably wouldn't help matters any.

Keisha placed her bag on the car seat and turned to pump her gas, but *Mr. Thug-body* was holding the pump smiling.

"I hope you use premium," he said, already inserting the nozzle. "So, you gonna tell the kid yo' name?"

"My name is Keisha, boy."

Her response was dry, yet her sly smile was fresh. It was early in the game, but Keisha was feeling dude's whole vibe. And judging from his outfit, which was classy, the brother had a little bit of paper. Crown Holder labels, nice Vizzie-link with diamonds and a $10,000 bracelet. And if that wasn't enough, the fool was whipping a brand spanking-new Benz.

"Keisha, huh? I think I like that name."

"Oh yeah, well, what's yo' name?"

"Nut."

Chapter 7
One Shooter – One Hoe-Nigga

"Man, that last brick I got from y'all was some *bling*, kid!" Bam said with excitement.

"This the same shit right here, kid-kid. We keep that *bling*."

BG and LG were selling two keys to Bam for $19,500 a piece. BG was expected to meet up with Frantz later that day to clear that *gangsta-tab*. He still owed the connect $40,000 from the five brick score he'd made at the Lexx, and these $39,000 from Bam would put him all the way in there.

"Everythang's everythang, bruh," LG said after counting the money.

Bam picked up his two kilos and left. No sooner than Bam cleared the doorway, JackBoy came out of the back room with his Mini-14 in hand. It wasn't that they didn't trust Bam, it was more like they only trusted each other.

"A nigga hungry, yo," JackBoy stated, rubbing his stomach.

"You're always hungry, nigga."

The three friends left together, heading to McDonalds on 62nd Street to get something to eat. As they rode, smoking *fire-green* and beating that *36 Ounces,* Plies mixtape, LG spotted a Lexus 430 cruising towards the projects.

"That's that nigga V-Dub right there!" LG yelled.

BG pumped his brakes and busted a quick U-turn. He was trying to catch the Lexus before it made it into the projects. JackBoy grabbed the Mini-14 off of the floorboard and prepared to get his man.

"Catch that booty-ass nigga!" LG yelled, .9mm in hand.

"I got 'im, bruh."

Surprisingly, the Lexus passed the projects and made a left turn on 2nd Avenue. BG had to be at least six cars back when the Lexus turned off. The light turned red as BG approached. *Not today!* he said to himself as he blew his horn and sped through the intersection, barely missing a collision with a Metro bus.

Flying down the street with the Lexus only four blocks ahead, BG saw his target make another left on 67th Street.

"You gon' lose the nigga, yo!" JackBoy screamed from the backseat.

"I got this, chill."

BG hit the left on 67th; the Lexus was parked in a church parking lot. JackBoy was out of the car before BG could make a complete stop. LG was right on his heels. They were twenty yards from the Lexus, guns aimed. The car doors began to open. Before they could let off a single shot, an older Haitian man, his wife and children, emerged from the vehicle. Upon seeing the *coming of death,* the Haitian man – wide-eyed and frightened – began yelling. "Amm'way! Amm'way!" Which translated, "Please don't killa muthafucka, please!"

JackBoy did not speak Creole, yet he understood. He and LG hauled ass back to the rental, hoping no one had seen their near blunder.

BG sped off, making a fast right off of 3rd Avenue, then a quick left onto 69th Street, which led to the *perfect escape route–* I-95. Just like that, the trio was Carol City bound.

3:00 p.m.

"We have got to get those damned *trouble-makers* off the streets," Detective Sims stated plainly.

He was at the Miami Dade County police station talking with his partner Detective Williams and two other officers from Vice. The topic was BG and LG. Sims and Williams had a real *hard-on* for BG. They'd been investigating several homicides in and around the Little Haiti area, homicides that they knew the twin brothers and their older cousin Gemo were involved in, but they couldn't prove it. Due to lack of evidence—a witness coming up dead, missing or simply changing their minds about testifying, had cost the state several cases. But not this time. Sims aimed to nail the brothers to the cross—for life.

"I'll have some of my very best men combing the area. And I'll be out there as well. They will not get away this time," said Captain Williams.

He then made the call. The brothers' days of running around killing were now numbered.

"Thank you, Captain," one of the officers said. "We finally have what we need to get them off the street and put them behind bars."

Detective Sims smiled brightly, he would finally have his day with the twins.

Exiting the station Sims got into his Crown Victoria and looked over the file that he'd been carrying. It was a new murder case. "Lord, Lord," the detective said to himself as he looked at the pictures of the slaying at a gas station, in Little Haiti.

Earlier the same day.

Bo-Jit left the trap on 55th Street and headed to his girl's apartment in the Grave Yard Projects. All that was on his mind was a nice shower, a *fire bag* of weed, some of his girl's *fire lip-service*, and some much needed rest. He'd been working like a madman keeping the traps up and running. *Damn, I'll be glad when BG 'em kill them chin-ass niggas so shit can get back to normal,* he thought as he rode. With them tied up in the beefing shit, it left all of the work on him, Teddy P and 50.

Bo-Jit made a quick stop at the Quick Stop. He needed a pack of Backwoods Sweet. The gas station sat on 71st Street and N. Miami Avenue, which was a main drag. So Bo-Jit paid no attention to the car that pulled in right behind him. It had been following him ever since he'd left the trap.

After paying for his Backwoods, Bo-Jit sat rolling him one. He wanted to be good and high when his *buss-it baby* got him right. Smiling, Bo-Jit fired it up, and the cannons exploded.

Boom! Boom! Boom! Boom! Boom! Boom! the dudes in the car that had been following him unloaded.

Bo-Jit only heard the first shot, it was a head shot. He died with his lungs full and a smile on his face...

¢ ¢ ¢

"What's up, kid? Shit must be boomin' if you callin' me this time of day," JackBoy said, feeling good.

Of course, that would soon change. The call was from Teddy P, and he was calling to let JackBoy know about his good friend Bo-Jit's murder. JackBoy was now speechless; he couldn't believe any of what Teddy P was telling him. He'd just talked to Bo-Jit before he left the spot heading to his girl's house.

"Man, JackBoy, the crackas was all over the gas station by the time I got there."

"How do you know it was kid? He coulda let somebody hold his car," JackBoy said, not wanting to believe what he knew was the truth. Bo-Jit never let anyone use his car... He was gone, and the shit hurt JackBoy so bad. The two were *real* childhood friends. From the dirt, before all the trap shit.

"I'm just telling you, kid. I hate that shit, too," Teddy P said sadly. "But they had to follow Bo-Jit from the trap, and caught 'im slippin' at the gas station."

JackBoy wiped the tears from his eyes and told Teddy P to shut the traps down. Shit had changed just that quick. They couldn't take any more chances with V-Dub and his team. They were hitting at them and knew where they trapped at. Their workers would be sitting ducks.

"How them *booty-ass, fuck-boys* know where we was eatin' at?"

"JackBoy, I don't know."

"Well, we gotta find out and close their shit for good."

Teddy P thought for a minute. "It can't be nobody we know, 'cause ain't nobody know that was our trap."

"Yeah, you right, yo. Call that lil' nigga 50. He might've been talkin' wit' them hoes and shit could've spilled."

"Nah, that lil' nigga ain't got no bitches, all he do is trap."

It may not have been 50, but they both knew that somebody had ran their *dick-suckers* and cost Bo-Jit his life. Now their job was to find them.

"Meet me at the *low-key* crib, ASAP."

"Aiight, JackBoy, me and 50 are on our way."

JackBoy couldn't wait for BG and LG to finish with their meeting. He needed to respond to the act committed against them. *Power responds to power!* So he planned to hit Edison Projects with everything that he had. V-Dub, Nut and their whole mob would pay dearly for touching one of his.

¢ ¢ ¢

V-Dub and Nut were *ducked off* at their stash-house in Robbin Hood. They both knew that retaliation for killing Bo-Jit was forever certain.

81

Nut was the actual shooter, and the events kept playing over in his mind. The echoes of gunfire and the blood and brains that flew all over the car's interior had Nut a little fucked up. He had killed before, however he'd never been close up and seen a man's entire brain exit his skull.

"Them *bitch-ass* niggas BG, LG and JackBoy are next, my nigga," V-Dub vowed.

He was really feeling himself, when for real, he was the *hoe-nigga* on the hit. He did not get out and had not done shit. Like Trick Daddy rapped on *THUG NIGGAS DON'T LIVE THAT LONG, I heard it was four killers, three shooters, one hoe-nigga! I'm out the pen' whatchu hidin' fo'?* The hoe-nigga driving was V-Dub and he was now hiding out.

The streets of Little Haiti knew all about the beef that was cooking between the two squads. After Doc had gotten murked, V-Dub went public. He made sure that everyone knew that his team would kill, too. He couldn't stand to be perceived as soft on the streets.

"Them boys gonna really be on point now, yo."

"Fuck them niggas. We'll catch 'em one by one, once a week, twice a month or all at fuckin' once! I don't give a fuck, Nut!" V-Dub yelled. "I ain't gon' let no niggas run me, then run and tell my uncle what they done to me."

Yeah, aiight, Juvy, Nut thought. But he knew that all hell was about to break loose. He was not sure if V-Dub fully understood that. As he thought about all of the drama that was sure to unfold, his phone rang.

"Hello?"

"Hey, Nut."

"Oh, what's up?"

"You... whatchu doin'?"

Keisha and Nut had been playing a lot of phone tag lately and they both liked it. Today Keisha wanted to see him in person. They had not seen one another since their very first meeting at the gas station that day.

Keisha invited Nut over to her place so that they could have a little dinner, talk, and get to know one another a little better. Nut agreed because he needed some pussy and couldn't stand to sit up with V-Dub for another minute.

"Yo, V, I'm out, kid."

"Where you headed, yo?"

"Lil' momma I met the other day wanna do me somethin' big, ya heard me?"

"She *rossin'* or what?" V-Dub asked excitedly. He loved to train other niggas' hoes and save his own.

"Nah, kid, baby lookin' like wifey."

V-Dub was disappointed, but Nut didn't give a fuck. He grabbed his weed and lace, car keys, and gun—leaving his partner hiding alone in the stash-house.

¢ ¢ ¢

It did not take Nut long to get to Keisha's apartment. High, dick hard, he stood at her door waiting for what he hoped would be an eventful night. He fingered the Glock .40 that rested in his pocket as he waited. Nut knew the game, therefore he never took chances when it came to visiting hoes.

The door finally opened, slowly. Nut wasn't sure what to expect. Ready for whatever, he almost shot himself in the leg when he saw what was waiting for him just beyond the threshold.

What the fuck?! he thought as Keisha stood naked. Not even saying hello, Keisha snatched Nut inside and slammed the door shut.

The two locked lips and exchanged grunts until they stumbled onto the couch. Keisha was all over Nut, sucking and touching. With each passing second an article of Nut's expensive outfit was torn from his body.

Now naked, Nut pushed Keisha's head down to his throbbing dick. Keisha admired the large sex-muscle, kissed it once, and after looking Nut in the eyes for a second, she worked her magic.

With Nut's dickhead lost deep in her throat, Keisha snaked her long, fleshy tongue out of her mouth and onto his balls. She simultaneously sucked him off and licked his nuts. Nut tensed up and wiped away some tears that had begun to fall from his closed eyes.

Lord, help me... I done fell in love wit' a ross, he thought.

Keisha smiled inside. She knew she had him. Dick still in her mouth, her tongue softly stroked his nuts. Nut was now bucked up with Keisha's index finger in his ass. He'd never felt such pleasure.

"Oooh, shi-shit," he moaned.

Keisha was massaging his prostate gland and he loved it.

"Ba-by, wait," Nut begged as what felt like a gallon of thick, rich semen ran from his body.

Keisha caught and swallowed every drop of it. Still dropping her head and applying pressure, Nut could not take any more. He roughly pushed Keisha off of him. She fell backwards onto the floor with her legs wide open. Nut stared at her moist insides.

"Boy, I know you ain't runnin' from me?"

"Girrrl, damn."

Keisha jumped up and came at Nut headfirst, like a soccer player. She was hell-bent on getting the *dope boy* sprung. With Nut's dick back in her sloppy wet mouth, Keisha worked her tongue, jaw and throat muscles until his manhood swelled to twice its normal size.

She quickly spat his dick out and climbed on it, taking it all like a *big girl.*

"Oh, shit, baby... I feel you in my stomach," Keisha moaned.

Nut held on to her fat ass and dug deep. Oblivious to the fact that he was up in her raw. That was something he never did on the first night. But he was gone. He had to be. He'd allowed a bitch to stick her finger in his ass.

"Oh, yes, baby... Oh, yes... Put it in my ass!" Keisha yelled.

Nut flipped her over with the quickness and claimed his prize.

"Oh, baby... I'm cummin', I'm cummin'," Keisha yelled as Nut rammed the full length of his dick in her gaping asshole.

Keisha felt her cum deposit empty all at once, skeeting out like an infant spitting milk. Her legs trembled as the two laid stuck like dogs in a cold abandoned shed.

¢ ¢ ¢

Lil One and JackBoy sat in the Carol City hideout playing PS2 and waiting for Teddy P and 50 to arrive. It had been over an hour since JackBoy had spoken with Teddy P.

"Where the fuck is these niggas at?" JackBoy asked out loud. He was not at all interested in the game he was playing. He wanted to go out and shoot at real muthafuckas.

"They comin', bruh," Lil One replied coolly. "You wanna pill?"

"Nah, fool," JackBoy said and walked over to the window.

Two police squad cars mobbed up the block followed by an unmarked.

"Fool, check this out!"

Lil One washed his pill down with some orange juice and walked over to the window. The D.T. car was just turning the corner.

Thinking that 50 and Teddy P might've had to run the *crackas* and jump out, they both got in Lil One's LTD and combed the block. The homies might've been *out there bad* and in need of a ride.

As the two bent corner after corner, they saw that the police were riding extra hard. They were pulling cars over and stopping people as they walked the street. Lil One noticed that the cops had a photo that they were questioning people about.

"They're definitely lookin' for somebody, bruh," Lil One slurred.

"Yeah, I just hope it ain't them boys, yo."

The two saw that there was nothing that they could do, so they headed back to the house. As they hit the street leading to Lil One's crib, red and blue lights flashed behind them. Lil One pulled over to the side of the road. They sat there as the cop waited for backup to arrive.

"You 54, right?" JackBoy asked Lil One.

"You think I woulda pulled over if I wasn't?"

Within a few minutes three more patrol cars pulled up. The officer of the original car got out and approached the car. His hand was on the butt of his service revolver.

"Roll down your window and place your hands out, now!" the scared officer yelled.

JackBoy took one look at Lil One, who already had his hands and head out of the window, and began letting his window down. By the time he placed his hands out there was another officer on his side as well.

"Let us see some ID, please... and no sudden moves," the lead officer ordered.

After getting both men's ID, one policeman walked off to run them for warrants.

"What did I get pulled for? What's goin' on, sir?" Lil One asked.

"These damned tints are too damn dark for one," the policeman spat with more attitude than a whore when her period's on. "And we are also lookin' for a murder suspect. Either one of you boys kill anyone?"

"Not today, sir," Lil One said with a smirk.

Just then the other officer returned. "They're clean."

"So we're straight, right?" Lil One questioned the policeman.

"Not yet... Here, take a look at these photos. Have you seen these boys around here?"

86

Lil One looked at the picture and then looked at JackBoy.

"Nah, can't say I have, officer."

"Yeah, me either."

The officer put the picture of BG and LG, marked armed and dangerous, back on his clipboard and walked away.

¢ ¢ ¢

BG and LG had just left their meeting with Frantz. Because they'd handled their end of the business like true G's, and Frantz and ZoeMan really had love for Gemo, the twins left the meeting in possession of ten kilos. They were excited about the increase in their work load, and couldn't wait to hug the block. The two had seen some work before, but never ten at once.

"It can only get better, bruh," BG said as they rode.

"Yeah, but we gotta get this work off, A-sap."

"We gon' get it off, one rock, one ounce or one brick at a time. It's gon' go."

LG's cell phone rang before he could respond to his brother's statement.

"Yeah?"

"Yo, L, the crackas got y'all flick on some M-1 shit."

"What?"

"Yeah, by the hideout, too. So both of y'all better lay way low."

LG told Lil One and JackBoy to meet them at Ms. Gin's house. Shara's mother was an OG, so LG knew that it wouldn't be a problem to lay the bricks there for a minute or two.

"I'm on 95, I'ma turn around and meet you there."

"Aiight, me and JackBoy on our way."

Chapter 8
No Pressure

When everyone arrived at Ms. Gin's place they went to the backyard to talk. Lil One and JackBoy explained everything concerning the police stop and the heavy police activity around the hideout. Everything seemed to come back to one question, *Who was tipping the police off?*

"Well, look, we all need to get new phones. All of the people that we used to call, don't call 'em no more, not on these new phones," BG ordered.

LG was also supposed to change out the rentals. BG did not want to take any chances with the cops pulling one of their vehicles because someone had pointed it out. They had to cover their tracks, at least until they found the leak in their program.

"So what about the work?" JackBoy asked.

BG told him that everything would remain the same, as far as trapping. But until they got everything back in order he wanted the spot on 55th Street shut down. Teddy P and 50 would still run the other traps as usual.

"We ain't gon' stop gettin' money just 'cause the crackas trippin' and these *chins* gotta lil' *L*," BG explained.

"As for them *EP-ass* niggas, when the new whips come through we gotta do some major homework on them *chins,*" LG added.

All four men agreed. They all knew that getting money and war didn't mix too well. So they would have to get the *beef-shit* over with sooner than later. Because if they continued with the back and forth killing both sides would lose in the end.

After the meeting was over LG and BG stashed away eight of the ten kilos. 50 and Teddy P swung through to pick up two for the traps. Their plug had the best cocaine in Miami, and their beef was not going to stop them from rocking it down and distributing it.

¢ ¢ ¢

BG walked into the house and made his way to the bedroom. When he entered the room Keisha was laying naked in his bed. She looked so sexy, working the butterfly vibrator against her swollen clitoris. BG loved what he saw, but was totally confused as to what was going on.

"Keisha, what the fuck is you doin'?"

"Waiting for you, lover."

"How the fuck you get in here? And how the fuck you know where I stay?"

"I did my homework, baby," Keisha purred.

BG saw the wild, uninhibited glaze in her eyes and thought back on the *animal-sex* that they'd had in her apartment on his second day home. His manhood began to swell beneath his clothing. Keisha saw the growing bulge and smiled.

"I know you miss this *fire-ass* head, boy... You don't have to feel bad about how you feel," she said, slowly crawling to the edge of the bed where BG stood. "Missy was my girl, but this is beyond her."

Keisha snatched BG's pants down and magically worked his snake like an evil enchantress charming a King Cobra. BG just closed his eyes and held on to her bobbing skull. The feelings were like none he'd ever experienced. It was velvet, like Blueberry Cush in a Strawberry Swisha.

"Come on, ba-be," were the last words he heard before he found himself naked, laying across the bed with Keisha on top of him. They kissed passionately. From his lips to his stomach and back to his love-muscle, Keisha kissed and sucked. Her vagina was dripping like a candy waterfall. She loved what she was doing.

"Right there, Mis—" BG caught himself. "Ms. Keisha... right there, baby."

Slick ass nigga, Keisha thought, smiling. She'd heard him almost call her Missy, but she did not care. She was there and Missy wasn't. So she tried her hand. Turning around with BG's dick still in her mouth, she positioned them in a 69. BG was so caught up in the magic of Keisha's enchantment that he didn't even fight for his head. He simply began pleasing Keisha with all that he knew.

"Oooh, yeeesss! Shiid, baby! Hurricane, ba-be, hurricane!" Keisha yelled.

BG started twirling his tongue in a fast circle, striking the circumference of her gaping pussy and her clitoris in rapid succession.

"Ooooh, God! Yeeesss!" Keisha yelled as she came in the eye of the storm.

BG licked up every drop of her candy rain. From a Category One storm to a Category Five, BG worked his tongue and lips, but Keisha couldn't take it anymore. She rolled over onto her back and cried, "Fuck me, BG, fuck me, baby!"

BG rolled on top of her and slammed all ten-inches of his hard dick into her.

"BG... BG... BG...!" he heard a voice yelling.

He looked into Keisha's face. She was smiling an evil smile and her mouth was not moving.

"BG... BG... BG!"

He looked in the direction of the voice and saw a shadow in the darkness. It was the figure of a very shapely woman. She was pointing something in his direction, at him. He eased his dick out of Keisha and tried to get out of the bed, but Keisha grabbed his arm and held him.

"What's wrong, nigga? Don't get scared now," she said, laughing.

"BG, I can't believe you did me like this. I trusted you with my life and you betrayed me with this no-good bitch!" Missy stepped from the shadows, aiming a gun. "I loved yo' ass and you did me like this?" She cocked the hammer. "You can't trust no bitch, BG. Especially a bitch like Keisha... Do you hear me, BG... BG!" she screamed as she started shooting.

"BG... BG... Yo, BG!"

BG jumped up and looked around quickly. He was sweating like hell. After checking himself for bullet wounds he looked next to him for Keisha.

LG looked at him, laughing. "Boy, what the fuck is wrong with you? First, yo' ass was dry humpin' the bed, then you was tryna jump outta that bitch! What's up, kid?"

BG shook his head. "Fuck you, nigga."

"Nah, you look like you done did all the fuckin' already, bruh. You might wanna check yo'self before we leave. So hurry up!" LG said, still laughing.

They had to go and pick up Shara and her sister to get the new rental cars. The day would be a long day, so they had to get an early start.

¢ ¢ ¢

V-Dub met his uncle's right-hand man at a pool hall in North Miami Beach. It was a quick meeting. V-Dub owed some money from his last shipment and also needed to re-up. He hated being out in the open with all the beef he had cooking. Of course, his uncle had no idea and V-Dub planned to keep it that way.

"So what's goin' on with you in these streets?"

"Whatchu mean?" V-Dub asked as he handed his uncle's man the money bag and received the big duffle bag in return.

"I mean, I hear things. Doc got murdered. You have not been around in your spots, some are closed down. What's goin' on?"

"It's nothin', a little misunderstanding, that's all. Business is good, ain't no pressure," V-Dub lied. The pressure surely was on. He had to kill BG and LG before the shit got too out of hand or got back to his uncle.

"No pressure, huh?" his uncle's man said, eyeing him. He knew that V-Dub was lying. He also knew that the youngster had an enormous ego, so there was no questioning whether V-Dub wanted to handle his own business or not. "Be careful, V-Dub, and see it through to the end."

"I got this, man... no pressure."

The two men got back into their respective rides and went about their business...

¢ ¢ ¢

"Boy, where your ass been? 'Cause I thought you was tryna buck me, boy, for real."

"Nah, *baby-girl*, I would never do no shit like that," LG explained to Black Barbie. He knew that she was a real bitch and could be dangerous. He needed to establish a relationship with her. One like she shared with his cousin Gemo. "Check this out, Black, I might need you again."

"Well, that's cool, LG, but I need my money."

"Money? Look here." LG went into his pitch. All he really needed was some intel on Nut or V-Dub, because it seemed that the two of them had disappeared. LG knew how hoes were, they were nosey and valuable. Nine times out of ten, a bitch knew something and had talked about it to her gossiping-ass partners.

"You know what?" Black Barbie said, snapping her finger. "I think my friend fuck wit' the dude V-Dub."

"Well check it out for me and get back at me if you hear somethin'."

Barbie thought about the shit. She'd heard that the nigga V-Dub and his crew were some *head-bussers*. Still, LG was Gemo's cousin, so he had to be a one-hundred percent real nigga. "Look, by the time you brang me, me, I should have heard somethin'. So put that lil' money together with somethin' extra for this here."

"Aiight, I'ma see you at eight o'clock then."

"Nah, make it nine, I got shit to do."

"How 'bout you just call me when you're ready to meet me."

"Yeah, that'll work."

LG hung up happy that he'd successfully added Black Barbie to his team.

¢ ¢ ¢

"I know you heard 'bout Bo-Jit," JackBoy said.

"Yeah, man, that was fucked up," Sunny answered, being the true snake that he was.

Still playing both sides of the fence, he told JackBoy about a stash-house that he'd heard Nut talking about in Robbin Hood. Nut, just as crazy as his name implied, had taken Sunny there once to fuck some bitches. "It's a peach and white house, you can't miss it."

JackBoy smiled a mischievous grin as he pictured the possibility of catching Nut and V-Dub slipping and murking their asses. "I'm gon' have to check that out, yo," he said, passing Sunny half a stack for the information.

"Shiid, it ain't no pressure, big homie. I fuck wit' y'all." Sunny pocketed the money. "Y'all boys just break the kid off somethin' if y'all *lick*."

"I gotchu, kid, 'cause this shit here is bigger than Nino Brown."

JackBoy dapped Sunny up and jumped into his rental. Limo tints, Mini-14 on his lap, JackBoy picked up his cell phone and called BG. BG hit LG on the three-way.

"Kid, we might just have our man."

"Run it down."

"That kid, Sunny—he gave me a Robbin Hood address on ya boy 'em."

"How Sunny know about the house?" BG asked.

"He told me somethin' 'bout ridin' through and peepin' V-Dub's *slider* posted up 'round there or some shit."

"Well, I'm on 95th Street right now. I can ride through right quick and check it out," LG said.

The whole situation sounded crazy to BG. For all he knew it could've been a setup. However, he was not willing to pass up an opportunity to kill V-Dub.

"Go ahead and slide by there," BG finally said.

"What color is the crib?" LG asked.

"Peach and white, yo," JackBoy answered.

The phone line went silent as LG scanned the block.

"Aiight, I see that shit. It's on the left side of the street, comin' off 17th Avenue."

"That's it, kid."

"Aiight, yo, tonight we ride. We gon' show 'em it's straight pressure over here," BG stated and they all hung up.

¢ ¢ ¢

"Hello?" Keisha answered her phone.

"Hello, Ms. Jones, how have you been?" Detective Sims asked.

Peaches and cream, cracka! Keisha wanted to say, but instead questioned, "What do you want now?"

"What do I want? Keisha, I thought we were friends."

"Well, you thought wrong," Keisha snapped. She was truly tired of them fucking with her.

"Your boy has not been showing up on the GPS system."

Ever since BG had gotten rid of his old cell phone, the police had lost him. They didn't have the frequency to his new phone, so tracking him was impossible. That was their bad because they could have picked up BG when they first started tracking him. Yet they wanted to wait for him to retaliate against Missy's shooters, and use the GPS signal to prove that he was on the scene. Of course, they hadn't planned on him changing phones.

"Look, maybe y'all just need to upgrade y'all's shit," Keisha sassed the detective.

"No, maybe you need to get out in the streets and find him," Detective Sims corrected her. "You haven't forgotten our little agreement now, have you?"

Keisha hadn't forgotten. She didn't want to go to jail, nor did she want to lose her children. There was a deep hatred for Detective Sims and all *crackas* like him that filled Keisha's heart. But the lies that they'd fed her had her scared to death. "I, I haven't heard anything from him though, sir. I—"

"You what?" Detective Sims cut her off. "You get out there and find 'im!"

"But, how I'ma do that?" Keisha whined. She was so lost and so sorry that she'd ever gotten involved with them.

"*How* isn't the issue. It's *when*, Ms. Jones. Now go and find that asshole!"

The phone slammed in Keisha's ear before she could say another word...

Part 2WO

"...a feared enemy must be crushed completely. If one ember is left alight, no matter how dimly it smolders, a fire will eventually break out. More is lost through stopping halfway than through total annihilation... Crush him, not only in body but in spirit."

— Robert Greene

THE ENDING

Chapter 9
Jackpot

The phone rang at 1:00 p.m. sharp. BG was laid back pondering over his next move. It seemed that nothing he'd planned had gone right. Abandoning his thoughts, BG finally picked up the phone.

"Yeah?"

"This is a pre-paid call from a federal correction institution, you will not be charged for this call...This call is from '*Gemo the Kid*'... Press five to accept this call... press seven to—"

BG quickly pressed five, cutting off the stupid automated operator and connecting him with his big cousin. "What's up, cuz?"

"Shiid, what's up wit' you? I hear y'all kids terrorizin' the streets."

"Nothin' but pressure, cuz. Ain't nothin' we can't handle."

"I hear you, cuz. Just don't be out there playin' wit' niggas. Get money, kid."

"A nigga ain't got time to shu-shu. I'm for real out here, you feel me?"

Gemo was plugged into the streets heavy, so there wasn't much that he didn't hear or know about. Even on the inside, news from the streets travelled fast. Especially with him having Black Barbie on his line, Gemo stayed abreast of everything.

"Yeah, I feel you." Gemo paused to think about his next words. He knew that they would sadden his little cousin, yet he had to tell him. "Yo, kid, I lost my appeal."

Silence. "Damn, cuz, that's fucked up," BG said sadly. "What about a rehearing?"

"Right now, I'm like fuck all that shit. I only have a few more years to go, anyway. So I ain't 'bout to keep payin' lawyers and stressin' 'bout that shit. You feel me?"

"I guess, kid... What about yo' girl, she know? She gon' ride?"

"Kid, Danielle ain't goin' nowhere, that's my ride or die right there."

"This is a call from a federal correctional institution," the automated operator said, interrupting their conversation.

"Man, why that stupid-ass *computer-hoe* keep sayin' that stupid shit?" BG asked.

"I don't know, kid. I guess they don't want a nigga to forget that he's socially deceased and at their mercy as long as we are on this end of the phone line."

Silence. Gemo's statement really fucked BG up, because it could just as easily been him calling Gemo from the other side. He thought about all the things he took for granted and so foolishly put on the line for money, his life and his freedom being the most costly.

"You still there, kid?"

"Yeah, I'm here, cuz... and yeah, befo' I forget, I got that bread for you."

"Cool, just give it to Black Barbie for me, she knows what to do."

BG knew why Gemo always had him to give his money to Black Barbie instead of his wifey Danielle. Barbie was a street bitch from the word go, that he could never change. Whereas Danielle was a grade-A square, and he didn't want to change that by involving her in his business, in any way. He knew that if she knew nothing, she could tell nothing. The Feds played raw. They would lock up your mother to make you *rat-out* your man.

"Me and LG was gon' slide through and see you, but you already know what's up."

"Yeah, I heard 'bout that. I'ma holla at a few people and find out who's who for you."

"Aiight, do that for me."

"No pressure, cuz. But check this out, these people done called chow, so I'ma holla at you later, kid."

"Aiight, one."

"Hundred."

¢ ¢ ¢

Keisha and her new dude Nut were laid back off of the *fire-green* and drinks watching *Friday* on DVD at Keisha's apartment. The two lovebirds had truly been enjoying each other.

"That nigga Chris Tucker is a fool, for real."

"He sho' is crazy, bay," she responded, smiling and chinky-eyed.

Keisha felt really good, not only because she was drunk and high, but because she was really feeling Nut. Being with him not only helped her financially, but it helped her forget her legal problems.

Nut, on the other hand, was completely gone. Keisha had his nose wide open. After their first *sex-a-thon*, he pretty much moved in with her and her two children. They loved Nut as much as he loved their mother.

As they laid there cuddled, someone knocked on the door. Keisha prayed that it wasn't her sorry-ass baby-daddy or the damned police.

"Somebody at yo' door, lil' momma," Nut said, looking crazy.

"Boy, I hear it," Keisha replied, looking crazier.

The person at the door continued to knock, this time much harder.

"I'm comin', damn!"

Keisha's voice and strut was filled with attitude as she left her bedroom and neared the front door. She couldn't imagine who would be knocking at her door.

"Who is it?"

"Girl, open this damn door!"

Keisha immediately recognized BG's voice. *Damn!* she thought and opened the door.

¢ ¢ ¢

LG and JackBoy got together and came up with a plan to rob and kill V-Dub or whoever was at the stash-house when they got there. LG just wanted to kick in the front door with guns blazing, but JackBoy was against that. He wanted to lay on the house, watch how they moved in and out, then lay them down.

"So whatchu sayin' is, you wanna sit around and waste time?" LG popped slick.

"Look, kid, they don't call me JackBoy for nothin'. Just trust me, yo."

"Nigga, you sell dope."

"Yeah, I'm 360 in these streets. Kid, I do it all."

JackBoy and LG both got into their cars and headed to Robbin Hood. They didn't want both cars on front street, so JackBoy agreed to be the eyes while LG parked up the block as backup.

"Yo, LG, I'm on the opposite side of the street, three houses down, by the black and white house."

The spot was perfect. He could see the stash-house and everything that moved on the entire street. LG was parked down a little farther. He could not see the house, but he had a good view of JackBoy's car, and could also see anything that moved in that direction. All they had to do was wait for someone to come or leave the house.

"Look here, JackBoy, I ain't gon' be out here all day, yo," LG said over the phone.

"Fall back, kid. We gotta wait. We don't know who's in there or how many."

That was LG's only flaw, he had no patience. JackBoy spent more time on the phone calming him down than he did watching the house. And when it was all said and done, the only thing that had changed in LG's mind was he wanted to kick in the back door instead of the front.

"You're a fool for real, LG."

"Yo, a fool is what a fool does."

"What?"

As JackBoy considered LG's statement, LG spotted V-Dub's Lexus creeping down the block.

"Yo, JackBoy, fool's Lexus is comin' past you!"

JackBoy looked just as the car passed him and pulled into the driveway of the stash-house. JackBoy watched carefully as V-Dub got out of the car and made his way to the front door. His eyes were locked on the man's every move.

Never did he see or expect to see LG creeping down the street. LG continued at a snail's pace until he was close enough to do his thing. In one hand he had a Mini-14, while a Glock .40 rested on his waistline.

What the fuck...? What is kid doing, JackBoy asked himself as he finally spotted LG creeping up on V-Dub.

LG was now ducked down behind V-Dub's Lexus, using it for cover, while he waited for V-Dub to open up the front door.

"Fuck!" JackBoy said as he hopped out of the car and began jogging up the sidewalk. He only hoped that he made it there before LG made his move, because despite what anyone else thought, he knew that V-Dub was dangerous. *This nigga got me*

101

out here, big fi' in my hand, in broad daylight, JackBoy thought to himself as he continued on.

V-Dub opened the door and peeked inside before walking in. LG made his move. V-Dub's back was turned to him, and by the time he heard the footsteps...

¢ ¢ ¢

"What are you doin' here, BG?" Keisha asked, hands on her hips.

"I came to holla atcha, what's up?"

Keisha just looked at his fine-ass. She was a bit nervous because of the circumstances. *I sho' wish Nut's ass wasn't in my muthafuckin' room right now. 'Cause I would give BG the red light special,* she thought. Keisha was unaware of the beef brewing between BG and Nut. She had slept with her best friend's man, and was now sleeping with the man that helped put her best friend in a life-threatening coma.

"This is a real bad time, BG."

"Why is that?"

"'Cause I got company."

BG's only reason for stopping by was to talk to Keisha about Missy's condition. He wanted to know had Keisha been to see her and whether anything had changed. Of course, the thought of Keisha sucking his dick had crossed his mind, but remembering the crazy dream that he'd had, he wisely pushed the thought aside.

"My bad, lil' momma, but I just wanted to know if you went to see Missy."

Hearing Missy's name made Keisha feel bad and a little angry. She thought for sure that BG was there for her *bomb sex.*

"Nah, I haven't... I've been real busy," Keisha answered with attitude.

"Aiight then, I'll see you later."

Keisha thought about Detective Sims' threat. "Hold up, BG, let me get yo' new number."

New number? BG thought. *How this bitch know I got a new number?*

His facial expression must have said exactly what was on his mind, because Keisha smiled and capped, "Boy, I've been callin' yo' phone, but it kept sendin' me straight to voice mail. So I knew you either had a new phone or you been duckin' me."

The shit sounded good and made plenty of sense, but BG wasn't sure. Missy had said not to trust her in his dream. And he had told his crew not to give or call anyone with the new numbers. It was his rule and he couldn't break it.

"Yo' number still the same?" BG asked.

"Yeah."

"Good, I'll call you later tonight."

With that BG turned and left. Keisha closed the door relieved, and headed back to her bedroom. Nut was laying there waiting.

"Who was that?" he asked. He'd heard the male voice.

"Nobody," Keisha answered simply.

Nut sat up. "Nobody, huh?"

"Boy, do not start. That was just the repairman asking about the damn AC he fixed the other day. Ookay?" she lied.

"Yeah, aiight." Nut halfway believed her.

"Jealous ass," she mumbled under her breath and laid down to finish watching the movie.

¢ ¢ ¢

"Oh, shit!" V-Dub involuntarily shouted when he turned around. The door was open and he had a fully-automatic AR-15 laying on the couch, but there was no way he would ever make it beyond the doorway with the two big gun barrels already aimed at his head. He'd been caught slipping. And judging from the looks in the two gunmen's eyes—both of which he knew—he was going to die because of it.

"Long time no see, homie," LG said.

He then pushed V-Dub into the house. JackBoy closed and locked the door. Once they were all inside, JackBoy held V-Dub at gunpoint while LG searched the house. He checked every room for anyone else that may have been in the house.

"It's clear, JackBoy."

"Find somethin' to tie this *chin* up wit'."

LG quickly tore the bed sheets and tied V-Dub up facedown in the living room.

"Where that work, nigga?"

"I ain't got no—"

Crack! the butt of JackBoy's .45 sounded against V-Dub's skull.

"Where that work at, nigga?"

V-Dub knew that he would die today, in this very house. Nonetheless, he couldn't stand another blow from JackBoy's iron. He had to say something. Anything. In order to delay his death and possibly save his life.

"It's in the back room, under the dresser."

It didn't take long to recover the two duffle bags from beneath the dresser. LG placed the bags next to the owner, who was still bound by his own bed sheets.

"Thanks for the donation, homie."

LG opened the first duffle bag and found that it contained stacks upon stacks of *gangsta* money. The second bag had fifteen kilos of cocaine in it. JackBoy and LG smiled, they had hit the jackpot.

"What we gon' do wit' kid?" JackBoy asked.

LG looked at him as if he was crazy. "Fuck you mean, *what we gon' do wit' kid?* We gon' do what the fuck we came here to do."

LG stood up with the Mini-14 in his hand and murder in his eyes. He kicked the two duffle bags aside and unloaded. *Boom!*

Boom! Boom! Boom! Boom! Boom! Boom! he pumped the whole drum into V-Dub's face. It would definitely be a closed casket.

Chapter 10
What's Done Is Done

Three days had passed since V-Dub's murder. JackBoy got word from Sunny as to where the funeral was being held. BG figured that this would be the opportune time to finish off V-Dub's entire crew. So the four of them—BG, LG, Lil One, and JackBoy all suited up in black Dickies, ski masks and big guns.

"I'm drivin' this time," BG said as they approached the *splack*.

Once everyone was inside the stolen Chevy Tahoe, BG headed for New Birth Baptist Church on 135th Street and 22nd Ave. With a Mini-14, two AK-47's and a MAC-11, the crew was heavily armed and ready for whatever.

"You see Nut's car?" BG asked as they pulled into the church's parking lot.

"Nah, just park, though. We'll see the nigga when everybody come out," Lil One slurred.

They all sat in the car on edge, listening to *gangsta* music... *help me father please 'cause I'm fallin'/ That's the Hennessey I hear callin'... Can I get some more / Hell 'til I reach Hell / I ain't scared / Momma checkin' in my bedroom / I ain't there... I gotta head wit' no screws in it / What can I do...* Tupac leaked from the speakers while murderous thoughts ran through each mans' mind.

Suddenly people began to file out of the church. The gunmen watched as the pallbearers came out carrying V-Dub in his eternal home. To their surprise, Nut was not one of them.

"Kid ain't even come to his man's funeral," LG acknowledged.

"Nah, yo, that nigga gotta be here," BG replied, praying that Nut was indeed there.

The men continued to watch and wait. BG refused to leave without getting his man. He had to have Nut today. That would complete his coup of V-Dub's crew and all of Little Haiti would be his.

Once everyone was out of the church and into their vehicles, the hearse pulled off and everyone followed.

"Let's hit it, BG," LG said.

"Nah, yo, hold up."

BG waited a few more moments then joined in with the procession of cars following the hearse. LG looked at his brother and saw that look in his eyes. He knew what BG was doing was crazy, yet he also knew that there was no reasoning with him, so he sat back and enjoyed the ride.

The graveyard where V-Dub was set to be planted was only a stone's throw from the church—it was on 125th Street near Pepper Park. BG parked the car and again the waiting game commenced. They watched as the sharply dressed pallbearers carried the great, now late, ghetto general to eternity.

"There go Nut right there!" someone in the Tahoe yelled.

BG wasn't sure who said it, because he was caught up in his own thoughts, wondering about his big day. Who would be his pallbearers? Would as many people show up for him? Would Missy be there? And would it be four dead-serious killers stalking his ceremony in hopes of eradicating their crew?

BG watched Nut close the door of the limousine that he'd just emerged from. He was fresh to death.

Big guns *click-clacked* as the men all chambered and readied their rifles for the assault.

LG had his door open and was about to explode when BG grabbed his arm.

"Wait!"

LG looked at his brother, confused. "Wait for what? We came to kill the nigga, there he go right there. Let's go kill 'im."

BG didn't respond to his brother's comment, he just continued to stare in Nut's direction. What he was seeing really had him fucked up.

"What's up, bruh?" LG asked.

Still no reply from BG. Nut was talking to a man that he respected, and for the life of him he could not figure out what the hell the man was doing at V-Dub's funeral, talking to Nut. With no answers to his questions, BG put the Tahoe in drive and pulled away.

"Bruh, what the fuck is you doin'?" LG asked.

BG shook his head sadly and slammed his closed fist into the dashboard. "Yo, that was ZoeMan that Nut was talkin' to!"

"What?"

"Yeah, ZoeMan," BG repeated, wondering what the fuck was going in.

¢ ¢ ¢

ZoeMan was really hurting on the inside. V-Dub's murder was a very big loss to the Haitian mob boss. Nonetheless, he looked strong on the outside as he and Nut talked. Nut's words were of comfort. ZoeMan liked Nut a lot. Yet he was more concerned about who had killed his sister's only son, V-Dub.

"So tell me, my young friend, who did this to my nephew?"

"It had to be BG and his crew."

When ZoeMan heard BG's name he couldn't believe his ears. BG was his good friend, Gemo's little cousin. He'd been doing business with BG. ZoeMan was puzzled. BG couldn't have had anything to do with his nephew's murder. And if he did, he couldn't have possibly known that V-Dub was his nephew. He planned to have Frantz set up a meeting.

"This BG, I know him," ZoeMan said softly.

"You do?" Nut was surprised. He immediately put two and two together and knew that that's where BG was getting his dope from.

"Yes, I did business with his cousin, Gemo... Now I do business with BG," ZoeMan confirmed Nut's theory.

Seeing his right-hand man in the distance, ZoeMan waved Frantz over. Once he got there ZoeMan explained the situation. Frantz couldn't believe what he was hearing. It was BG that V-Dub had been warring with, and he'd been serving him the whole time.

"I'll take care of this for you, Zoe," said an upset Frantz. He then turned to Nut. "Tell me everything you know about BG, where can I find him?"

Frantz was more enraged than ZoeMan. V-Dub was like a little brother to him. He listened with tight jaws and clenched fists as Nut detailed the entirety of the circumstances surrounding his best friend's murder. Nut broke down twice as he narrated the story, because he felt that V-Dub's death was in part his fault. Had he not been so enchanted by the sexual prowess of Keisha, he would've been there to save his dog... Or at least had the pleasure of dying with him.

After Frantz finished with Nut, he got on his phone. He placed two calls, one to his best and most trusted henchman and the other to...

¢ ¢ ¢

After leaving the graveyard BG, Lil One, LG and JackBoy headed to the little efficiency that they had in Wynnwood on 34th Street and 4th Avenue. No one would ever think to look for them in Wynnwood.

Lil One was the one to ask the question that everybody wanted to know. "So what we gon' do 'bout Zoe?"

BG said, "Man, I don't know, but I know he knows what's happenin' by now."

"So what we gon' do?"

"Fuck you mean what *we* gonna do?" LG butted into the conversation. "We gon' do what we programmed to do, we gon' war. That's what we gon' do. ZoeMan bleeds just like us."

BG heard his brother and he felt him. Yet he also knew exactly what would happen if they were to engage in an all-out war with ZoeMan. He had to really think this one out. Gemo's connect was now disconnected and he could possibly be in danger if ZoeMan decided to go after him. BG had to somehow get word to Gemo as to what was happening.

"I feel you, bruh... But for now, we gotta stay the fuck off the streets," BG finally said. He was fully aware of just how powerful ZoeMan was. His money was long as train smoke. So it would be nothing for him to put $100,000 on each one of their heads. No one in Little Haiti—not even friends and family—would turn that type of money down.

As BG sat pondering his next move, a cell phone went off. It was his. "Hello."

"BG... What's with you, my friend?"

BG demurred momentarily, then answered. "You know me, gettin' that money."

Frantz laughed a little. To BG it sounded like a snake's hiss. Frantz wanted to meet up with BG to *talk business.* Of course, BG peeped that it was a setup, still he agreed to meet him, he had no choice.

"How about we meet on 60th and NE 3rd Avenue?" Frantz suggested.

BG thought about the meeting place. It was the perfect place to ambush a muthafucka. The area was full of warehouses, and not too many people would be there around six p.m. Still, BG had no choice but to accept. "I'll be there, Frantz."

"Good, because ZoeMan really likes you, and asked that I take care of you."

"Oh, he said that, huh?" BG popped and looked at the phone. *This bitch-nigga must really think I am stupid,* he thought to himself. *ZoeMan don't even know me like that.*

"Yes, he said that and I aim to do just that. So make sure that you are on time. You know how I am about being on time."

"Yeah, I know. I'll be there, yo."

BG terminated the call. His facial expression said that it was time to *ride or die*. LG read the expression and nodded his head yes, reassuring his big brother that he was with him all the way.

Lil One was the first to speak. "What he say?"

"He wanna meet up at six o'clock on 60th and 3rd."

"So we gon' meet him, right?"

"Hell nah!" BG answered Lil One. "I just told that nigga that shit to feel him out. I know that shit is a trap and I ain't walkin' into it!"

Lil One smiled and shook his head. "Check this out, bruh," Lil One said and went on to explain his position. Since Frantz wanted to cross them, he told BG how they could beat him with the double-cross.

After listening to Lil One's plan, everyone in the small room was now smiling. "That shit just might work, yo. They think we green to what they're doin'," LG said.

"Shiid, I'm down, kid," JackBoy added.

"Well let's make it happen," BG said and they all got up and headed out.

¢ ¢ ¢

Keisha sat in her apartment watching reruns of *Daddy's Girls* on MTV. This was now her life—smoking the best weed, watching TV all day and fucking Nut all night. Since they had hooked up and made their relationship exclusive, Nut had taken on all of her bills and allowed her to quit her job. Keisha loved it. And she was starting to love Nut. At first all she wanted from him was some money and some good dick. But after getting both and seeing how he treated her and her children, she was finding herself wanting more love.

Just as Keisha was about to pick up the phone and call her knight in shining armor, it began ringing. She smiled brightly and hoped that it was him.

"Hello," she answered excitedly.

"Ms. Jones, how are you?" Detective Sims returned. "You seem pretty upbeat today. Is it beca—"

"I have not heard from him!" Keisha cut him off with much attitude.

"No, Ms. Jones, I'm sorry, I wasn't calling you about that." The detective paused. "I called to inform you that... your friend, Ms. McDonald, has passed."

Keisha covered her mouth with her free hand to stifle the shriek that wanted to escape. She shook, not wanting to believe what she'd heard the detective say. Tears ran down her face as thoughts of Missy crossed her mind.

"Not my friend, no—not Missy!" Keisha screamed.

"I'm sorry, Ms. Jones... I truly am... But we both know who's the blame here. Help me make him pay for what he's done to Missy... and to you."

Keisha thought about Sims' statement and in her emotional state it was easy for her to accept it as truth. "You, you're right... It, it is his fault... She's gone, Mr. Sims, she's gone," Keisha cried out.

Detective Sims smiled. He had Keisha right where he wanted her. "Ms. Jones, I'm so sorry, and this may not be an ideal time to question you concerning BG, but I really want him to pay for hurting you. So, maybe you may need to get with whoever you may know and find something out."

Detective Sims was right, it wasn't the ideal time because Keisha was not in the mood to play *Queen Snitch*. "Not tonight, Mr. Sims... My friend just died."

Damn! Detective Sims thought. *The bitch is dead and stinking, for crying out loud. Let's frickin' move on.* But said to Keisha, "I totally understand, Ms. Jones, but please give me a call when you're feeling better."

"I will," Keisha said and hung up the phone as Nut walked into the apartment. He saw that Keisha was crying and immediately made his way to her side.

"Damn, baby, what's wrong?" Nut asked, full of concern.

"My, my friend...she, she died today." Keisha bussed out crying even harder.

Nut hugged her tight. "I'm sorry to hear that, baby. What happened to her?"

"She, she got —" Keisha tried to explain, but the words would not come out.

She cried and shook uncontrollably as Nut held her.

"Easy, baby. It's okay, get it out. It's gon' be alright."

¢ ¢ ¢

Gemo was on the phone with Black Barbie getting the 4-1-1 on everything that was popping on the streets. The most important being the situation surrounding V-Dub's murder. Barbie told Gemo, in code, that the streets were talking, and word was BG and LG had everything to do with it.

"I kinda heard about some beef shit," Gemo said.

But what he hadn't heard was that V-Dub was ZoeMan's nephew. When Black Barbie told him it totally changed the dynamics of the situation. He knew that his two little cousins would need some help if they were going to live through a war with someone like ZoeMan. And he knew exactly who to call for help.

"You still got the homie Hot Rod's number?"

"Who, that nigga from West Palm Beach?" Black Barbie questioned.

"Yeah, that's him."

"I got the number, what's up?"

Gemo told Black Barbie to call Hot Rod up and let him know all about the situation. He knew that he could count on his old friend to hold the situation down. Hot Rod was older than Gemo and was someone whom he looked up to and trusted.

After hanging up with Gemo, Black Barbie called Hot Rod.

"Yeah, I'm lookin' for Hot Rod, this you?"

"Who this?"

"Black Barbie, Gemo's lady."

"Oh, aiight, this Hot Rod. What's good?"

She explained everything to him, he listened closely. ZoeMan was somebody he'd heard horror stories about, but Hot Rod barred none.

"Tell my nigga I got 'im," he said simply and hung up.

¢ ¢ ¢

When six o'clock hit Frantz was at the meeting spot waiting. He had his hired gunmen strategically positioned in the bushes along the railroad tracks. Frantz had five gunmen in all and could not wait to hear their cannons explode.

Looking at the clock on his jeep's dashboard Frantz sighed heavily. It was 6:10. He picked up his cell and called BG.

"Yeah?"

"You are late," Frantz said with clear disconcertment in his voice.

"My bad, yo. I'm comin' up the street now," BG stated calmly, though he was extremely nervous about the meeting.

"Okay, come on. I'm in the silver Benz Jeep."

After hanging up, Frantz hit his high beams to alert his troops that their prey was just a few seconds outside of killing range. They pulled their masks down and readied their weapons as the headlights of BG's vehicle flooded the small street. Frantz smiled, *revenge is the sweetest joy next to gettin' pussy,* he thought. BG was now directly in the line of fire.

Doom! Doom! Doom! Doom! Doom! shots rang out from the bushes.

Frantz quickly reversed his jeep as not to get caught up in his own ambush.

Tat! Tat! Tat! Tat! Tat! Tat! more gunfire erupted, knocking paint off of BG's ride.

The car was totaled. Blood leaked through the doorjamb onto the street. Still, the five gunmen continued to unload their guns.

Frantz was long gone, leaving his men to all of the dirty work. The gun shots could be heard from three blocks away.

"Cease!" one of the gunmen yelled.

They all walked over to the car, the driver was dead. There were no other passengers in the car.

"Come!" he said, and they all ran off towards the bushes from which they had emerged. But before they could reach them.

Yak! Yak! Yak! Yak! Yak! Yak! Yak! Yak! two different AK-47's cut loose. Followed by the call of a Mini-14 and two Mac-11's. *Tat! Tat! Tat! Tat! Tat! Tat! Tat!*

The five men were killed instantly. They never stood a chance.

After the last shell had fallen to the street top, the six new killers turned and disappeared. They could hear the police sirens as they sped back to Wynnwood.

¢ ¢ ¢

"Damn y'all boys, I feel bad as fuck 'bout what I did to Pops," BG said sadly.

It was Pops—the crack-head—who had driven BG's car into the ambush and died as a result. BG had lied to the old man, telling him that someone he knew wanted some work done, so Pops had readily gone on the bogus mission. While BG, Teddy P, Lil One, LG, JackBoy and 50 were all camped out in a mini-van down the street, watching as Pops drove to his untimely death.

"Man, fuck Pops bassin' ass. That nigga was a custo and now he outta there. Shiid, we did him a favor, for real," LG said, half laughing.

LG was just like that, cold-hearted and loose. He just didn't give a fuck.

"Nah, kid, we set the man up to get killed," 50 said. He damn near had tears in his eyes.

"Better him than us, nigga! Shiid, somebody gotta live to get the bitches and the money, and tell everybody the story of how it happened." LG wasn't laughing anymore. He was seriously upset that niggas were feeling bad about using a crack-head. "This is war, my nigga, and Pops was a casualty. Pour out some liquor, put his picture on a T-shirt, whatever! Y'all actin' like some real bitches."

BG started to check LG, but he knew his brother was right. Pops was a casualty, and what was done was done. There was nothing that they could possibly do to fix it.

Chapter 11
On Some Kid Shit

Shara received a call from Missy's cousin, Muffin, informing her that Missy had died the day before. The news was not a complete shock, being as Missy had been in a coma for so long. The fact that she was dead played on Shara's mental. She felt so bad because she was right there at the party with Missy. She could have easily gotten shot instead of Missy. The thought sent chills down her spine.

Someone had to tell BG. Shara got herself together and called LG.

"Hello," LG answered out of breath.

"Boy, what the hell are you doin'?"

"Look, don't start that shit."

Shara started to *read his ass the riot act*, but that could wait for later. For now she had to deliver the sad news of Missy's passing. "LG—baby, Missy died."

LG didn't say anything, he couldn't. How was he going to tell his brother that the love of his life was no longer living? All BG had been talking about as of late was he and Missy getting away from the mean streets of Miami and raising a family.

"You there, bay?" Shara whispered.

"Yeah, I'm here," LG's voice cracked. "I'ma holla though, I gotta let kid know."

"Okay, bay. Please tell him I'm sorry and to be strong."

"Bye."

LG hung up the phone and looked at BG. He was sitting on the edge of the bed, lost in thought. It wasn't hard to figure out who BG was thinking of. LG did not want to be the bearer of bad news. They were already at war with a vicious Haitian drug lord. LG thought that the news of Missy's death might throw BG off point. Nevertheless, he had to tell him.

"Aye, bruh, check this out."

"What's up?" BG asked, looking up from his daze.

"We need to holla." LG put his arm around his brother's shoulder. "Let's walk outside right quick."

The two brothers walked outside. BG automatically sensed that something serious was bothering his twin, he knew exactly what it was.

"It's about Missy, ain't it, bruh?"

LG shook his head indicating yes.

"She's, she's dead, bruh?"

Once again, LG indicated yes. "Shara just called and told me," LG whispered. "But how did you know?"

"She told me," BG answered, looking straight ahead.

"Shara?"

"Nah, Missy. It was like a dream, but it was real, bruh. She told me bye, yo."

LG fired up a blunt, hit it twice and passed it to BG.

"In the dream, I was asleep and Missy woke me up... I was happy as fuck to see her. So we sat there talkin'. She was so pretty, bruh, she had a glow to her hair and skin... She knew about all the shit with me and Keisha, but she wasn't trippin'... She said that I really made her happy and that she was gonna miss me." BG hit the weed extra hard and continued. "So I was like, *what's up? Where you goin'?* She just smiled and told me that she would always love me. And, bruh, she turned and walked away... I called out, *Missy! Missy! Hold up, Missy!* But she would not turn back around. She walked down this golden road, laced with red rose petals... I tried to run after her, but my legs would not move...I told her that I loved her and she was gone."

"I'm sorry, bruh," LG told him.

"Nah, she's in a better place now. Nobody, not even me, can hurt her again. Feel me?"

LG admired his brother's courage and strength. Yet, he knew that he was hurting deep inside.

¢ ¢ ¢

"You mean to fucking tell me that you let some fucking street punk out-smart you!" ZoeMan yelled at Frantz.

ZoeMan had received a play-by-play of the whole episode that had taken place the day before. He did not like any of what he'd heard. The streets were saying that for someone on ZoeMan's level, he should not have been having such problems. BG and his young squad were truly tarnishing his status.

"Boss, somehow he knew. He knew that we knew, and he set us up," Frantz stated. He also could not believe BG's ability to strategically plan and execute. The young hoodlum had pulled one over on him. Had he not driven off when the shooting started he would have been slaughtered along with his hired soldiers.

"No, he did not set *us* up, he set *you* up! Now you must find him and fast!"

"I will get right on it, Zoe."

Frantz pulled out his cell phone as he exited ZoeMan's home. Time was of the essence. The longer it took them to kill BG, the more foolish they would look. A man that could not handle his personal problems could not be trusted to control the affairs of others.

As soon as he was in his car, Frantz dialed Nut's number. He prayed that Nut knew something that could help him find and eliminate BG.

"Yeah?" Nut answered.

He was laid back at Keisha's apartment watching a DVD of Jim Beam in concert.

"Nut, this is Frantz. Have you heard anything about our little problem?"

I heard them boys put that work in yesterday! Nut thought, and was glad that he was not there. Like Juvenile said, *I'd rather see it on TV than to see it in person, and have my fuckin' head all hurtin' when them 30's be burstin'.*

"Nah, Frantz, but I can holla at this guy I know. He always seems to know somethin' about somethin'."

"Do that, my friend, and get right back with me."

Nut did not reply, he just hung up and called Sunny, the *Street Rat*. If Sunny knew something, and he relayed the information to Frantz, he would be in good with ZoeMan's organization. He might even get the work that V-Dub used to receive.

"Hello?" Sunny answered.

"Sunny, boy, whatchu got for me?"

"Whatchu mean, *what I got for you?*"

"Bitch, just what I said! What's up wit' them *chins*, BG and 'em?"

"Oh!" Sunny checked himself and spilled his guts.

Sunny told Nut about a conversation he'd had with his cousin Pooh. Pooh had overheard Shara rapping recklessly with LG about laying low in Wynnwood. They were in Mrs. Jay's beauty salon when the conversation took place.

"You know the address?" Nut asked.

"Yeah, you want it?"

"What the fuck you think?"

Nut hated Sunny and every nigga like him. Still, he took down the information and thanked Sunny for a job well done. Now he had to report his finding to Frantz.

¢ ¢ ¢

BG got a phone call from Black Barbie about meeting up with Gemo's friend, Hot Rod, up in West Palm Beach. At first he bucked at the idea of leaving Dade County. He deemed himself a warrior by blood, therefore bloodshed was not something he was going to run from. Instead, he'd run at it, and be proud to go out in a blaze, because he had a special angel named Missy waiting on the other side.

However, Black Barbie wouldn't hear of it. She explained everything that Gemo had said, and went on to add her own two cents. When she finally finished lying and over exaggerating, BG found himself calling up Hot Rod.

The two talked briefly. BG hated the fact that he'd put himself and his men in such a vulnerable predicament. Not to mention his pride. He was not afraid of ZoeMan, however he agreed to leave Dade for Palm Beach County.

"I'll call you back when I get close."

"Aiight, BG," Hot Rod replied, and they both hung up.

¢ ¢ ¢

BG headed to *Choppa-Locka* with LG and JackBoy trailing him in another car. He had to stop on 134th Street and 30th Avenue to pick up Lil One before hitting the road. While driving, thoughts of Missy were heavy on his tired mind. For some reason, he picked up his phone to call Keisha, but thought better. When he pulled up to Lil One's people's house he blew the horn. Lil One came out smoking dirty.

"What's hood, bruh?"

"Ain't shit," BG replied dryly and went on to explain the dynamics of their plight.

Lil One hit the potent mixture of weed and cocaine and blew out the thick black smoke, causing BG to lower his window. He hated the smell of lace, but Lil One was his man, and lace helped him function under pressure.

They headed down 135th Street and caught I-95 North as BG and Lil One traded thoughts. Unlike BG, Lil One thought the move to Palm Beach was strategic, not cowardly.

"Bruh, you always reading that *Art of War*, *48 Laws* shit, but when it's time to apply it, yo' brain lock up..." Lil One hit the blunt again. "The 34th law of the 48, says *keep a nigga off balance and in the dark, never reveal the true intent behind yo' actions.* 'Cause if a nigga's clueless 'bout whatchu up to, he can't put up a defense, my nigga. If ZoeMan think you're runnin', he will relax because he will think you're pussy. Once he relaxes, we will come through and clear that shit out, feel me?"

Guide them far enough down the wrong path, envelop them in enough smoke, and by the time they realize your intentions, it will be too late, BG thought about Robert Greene's exact words. Both Robert Greene and Lil One were right.

"That's why I fuck wit' you," BG said.

"No pressure, bruh, you're my man." Lil One let down his window and threw the remainder of his blunt out. "So where in West Palm does Rod live?"

"In the Raw."

"What the fuck is the Raw?"

"Riviera Beach."

Being in the 561 would be a nice change of pace for everybody. Lil One had heard that West Palm Beach was a helluva party spot for dudes that popped heavy pills and played the strip club scene. He couldn't wait to hit Sugar Daddy's and the Mirage—*wide ass open!*

122

BG checked his rearview to see how far back LG and JackBoy were. To his surprise they were right behind him. The drive to West Nam Beach—as some of the young hoodlums called it—was only about an hour drive.

Seeing Blue Heron Blvd, BG exited and called Hot Rod.

"Yeah?"

"Yo, I just got off of 95."

"Aiight, come east to S Avenue and 26th Street."

"I know where that is."

"Aiight, I'll be outside. You will see a Crown Vic' on 26's wit' a blueberry pearl in the yard. You can't miss it."

When BG found the house, there were five men standing around the Crown Victoria. He parked, tucked his *heater*, and got out of the car. By the time he'd walked the short distance LG was at his side.

"BG and LG, right?" Hot Rod asked, eyeing the twins.

"Yeah, that's us, what's up?"

BG knew that the man he was speaking to was indeed Hot Rod. The 5'10", 175 pound, muscle-bound dude had a very distinctive voice. It was sort of high-pitched and raspy. Seeing him for the first time, baldhead with four gold-teeth to the top, BG thought he was a young nigga.

"These my niggas right here, Short Dog, JD, AJ and Triple J," Hot Rod introduced his men.

"What's good, y'all boys? These my niggas here, JackBoy and my main man Lil One."

The nine men all greeted one another and discussed BG's reason for being in the Raw. BG was sure to check the point that he was not running. Hot Rod totally understood the point of emphasis, because he'd once been a *baby gangsta* striving to make his mark. Of course, even as an OG, he'd never faced the type of pressure that a man like ZoeMan was sure to bring.

Hot Rod told BG of his strong relationship with Gemo, so it was *whatever* with him. BG and his men were welcome to *lamp* as

123

long as they needed. Hot Rod and his team had 6th Street in the choke hold, so BG could also move his work in their traps. When the time came to ride or die, Hot Rod assured BG that he would be there—*Choppa* in one hand, grenade in the other.

"We can talk about killin' these niggas and business later. For now, let's hit the happy hour at Sugar Daddy's," Hot Rod told everyone.

"That's what I'm talkin' 'bout!" Lil One yelled, ready to see some naked hoes. "Y'all boys got some pills?"

Sugar Daddy's was located on Military Trail, a big pink building with neon lights.

They parked VIP which was on the side of the club. Hot Rod paid everybody's entry and they headed straight to the bar. The DJ was spinning that *Five-Star Bitch* by Yo Gotti. He then announced, "Welcome to the stage, China Doll!"

China Doll came out working her jelly. She was a big booty red-bone with long black hair. Her eyes were so slanted that you could barely see her pupils. At 5'6" and 135 pounds, China was a doll for real. Bills rained down on her from every corner of the stage.

"Boys, I'm in love wit' a stripper!" yelled JackBoy when China Doll bent over, showing the entire club her beautiful pink pearl.

In his mind, along with most naïve tricks, she'd done that just for him.

China Doll continued to dance around the stage, making her luscious ass clap along to the beat. JackBoy was lost in her magic as he continued to make it rain. China smiled in his direction as the big face twenties, fifties and hundreds fell.

Sensing his opportunity, JackBoy waved her over. And to his surprise she came.

"I'm feelin' you, ma. What's up wit' a lap dance?"

China Doll smiled a seductive smile and snatched all of the money from JackBoy's hand and whispered, "I'm feelin' me, too... So meet me in the back when I come off the stage."

JackBoy blushed like a *cold sucker*.

"Look like yo' boy fucked up 'bout her," Hot Rod said.

"Ain't it, man," BG capped back.

The two of them enjoyed a good laugh, watching as JackBoy rushed off to the back of the club to meet China Doll. Everybody else was laid back drinking and pill-popping as the fine, naked women entertained.

"Hot Rod, check this out. I still gotta few bricks I need to move, yo," BG said, eye-fucking this badass white chick on stage.

"Shiid, I'll buy a few straight up, and you can move the rest on 6th."

"Yo' fools ain't gon' trip?"

"Bruh, it's plenty of money out there for all of us. You feel me?"

BG now understood why Gemo had them come up to West Palm Beach with Hot Rod. He was an ultra-good nigga for real. "Yeah, I feel you, kid."

"Kid? Where y'all get that New York-ass shit from, my nigga?"

"Nah, it ain't no NY-shit, yo. Kid is just a word we use in Lil Haiti to say, we gettin' money. We *Lil Haiti kids*, and y'all West Palm kids, 'cause we gettin' money, kid. We on some *kid-shit*, feel me?" BG explained, he was drunk, high and feeling it.

"I think I feel you... *kid*."

BG's phone lit up on the table. He recognized 50's number. Picking up the phone, he excused himself to answer the call...

¢ ¢ ¢

Two unknown men exited a BMW and approached the moderate three bedroom house in Wynnwood. After peeking through the front window, they began knocking. There was no answer. They then walked around back and spotted a neat little efficiency. The two men slowly and cautiously made their way to the front door. One of the men placed his ear to the door to see if he could hear anyone inside. There was no movement. The second man walked along the side of the efficiency until he found a window. He broke the window, entered the dwelling, and opened the door for his partner. The two men waited for their prey to step into their trap...

Two hours later.
"Kid, you seen the way the bitch was sweatin' the kid?" 50 asked, truly feeling his new status in life.

"How you know she wasn't sweatin' me?" Teddy P asked as he stuck the key into the lock.

"I know it was me 'cause *I* got the number, yo."

"Whatever, you swear you on some real *kid shit*."

Teddy P entered the little makeshift house first, followed by 50, and ran his hand over the wall looking for the light switch. He never got to it.

He ceased his search when the big Haitian behind the door jumped out yelling "freeze!" 50 tried to run out but another Haitian kicked the door closed and slapped 50 with his pistol. The blow sent 50 crumbling to the floor.

"Get up, you two, over on the couch!"

Teddy P and 50 did exactly what they were told to do.

"Which one of you is BG?" the taller Haitian asked.

"B-B, BG don't live here," a scared-ass 50 stuttered.

The big Haitian was 6'8" and 265 pounds of coal-black muscle and was blessed with a mug that gave little children nightmares. He stood there staring at 50, directly into his scared eyes, searching them for the truth.

"Call him, now," the man demanded.

50 looked at Teddy P to see what he should do. He found Teddy P with his head down, shaking it from side to side—indicating no. Teddy P already knew that they were both as good as dead. So there was no need to get BG killed also.

126

"We, we don't have… have the… the number." 50 tried his best to sound sincere.

The big Haitian smiled and looked to his sidekick, who had not spoken yet. He nodded to the smaller Haitian and without warning, *Boom!* the big .45 roared, sending Teddy P's blood everywhere. He was dead before his body hit the floor.

"Now, do you think you can come up with the number?" the big Haitian asked, smiling.

50 didn't even have to think about it. He quickly grabbed his phone and dialed BG's number. He was scared to death. Tears ran down his face as he thought of his mother. He wished that he would've listened to her. Because she was right, "This kid shit wasn't worth it."

"What's up, 50?" BG answered.

"B-B, BG, man, they—"

The big Haitian snatched the phone. "So, BG, we finally get a chance to talk. You are very hard to get a line on."

"Who the fuck is this?"

"I'm the man that's going to kill you like I killed your two friends," he said and gave his sidekick another nod.

Boom! 50 died and the line went dead.

¢ ¢ ¢

BG walked back towards the spot on the sofa that he'd shared with his men. He was wide-eyed and numb. 50's voice and the thundering boom of the shot that killed him echoed through his mind.

LG, who was at the bar sipping and tipping, noticed the void expression on his brother's face and hurried over to him. "What's up, bruh?"

"They killed them."

"They killed who?"

"50 and Teddy P."

127

"Who? Who killed them? When?"

BG told LG all about the phone call that he'd received. LG could see that his brother was truly fucked up. The killing of his friends and loved ones was starting to wear him down. Of course, LG was not bothered at all. 50 and Teddy P were his good friends, and he really cared about Bo-Jit and Missy, but he felt like *when it was your time to go, you're gone.* So he wasn't down, he was mad and thinking about payback.

"Something ain't right, bruh."

"Man, who you tellin'? First Missy, then Bo-Jit, now it's Teddy P and 50."

"Yeah, but it's bigger than them being dead, bruh. Somebody sellin' us out."

The brothers thought about it and discussed the events that led them to where they were; V-Dub shooting up the surprise party, the police tracking them to Carol City, V-Dub finding the trap on 55th Street, and Teddy P and 50 getting caught slipping. The whole situation did seem strange.

"We gotta get back, bruh," BG finally said.

"Shiid, we're out then."

They found Hot Rod making a hurricane with bills over by the stage. BG tapped him on the shoulder. "Thanks for the good time, but we gotta go."

"With all these bitches in here, *kid*. Let me find out!" Hot Rod replied.

BG chuckled a little at Rod's use of *kid*. "We got some problems back at the crib, and we gotta handle them, ASAP."

"Aiight then, y'all niggas be safe, yo."

LG went over and broke up JackBoy's private session with China Doll. JackBoy was reluctant at first, but once he saw the look on the twins' faces, he knew that something was seriously wrong.

"Damn, China, baby, I gotta go."

128

"But the song ain't over… and I wasn't through with you," she whined seductively.

"Yeah, but my niggas need me." JackBoy pushed her off of him. "And I never put a bitch before my friends."

She was about to frown up her pretty face when JackBoy pulled out a bankroll, peeled off three hundred dollars and passed it to her with his number.

"Thank you," she said and smiled.

JackBoy kissed her square on the lips and walked away…

¢ ¢ ¢

"…what we have here is a problem! A serious problem! With the Haitian man turnin' his wide nose up at the Black man, because in his mind he's concluded that he's not a Black man, but that he's better than the American so-called Black man… While the Black man, for his part, in his sick whitewashed mind, has used the title *Black American* to separate himself from his Haitian brother… Nigga, you're not American! And Joseph, Joel, Jolee Francois, you are just a nigga speakin' broken French… Yeah, a nigga! And we'll always be niggas to the crackas as long as we continue to let *language* and *Nationality* keep us separated as a people! When in reality neither the so-called American Black man or our so-called Haitian brothers are speakin' our original language or adhering to our original laws and culture, which comes from Mother Africa!" a fired up Arthur Cruz rocked a live audience filled with young Haitians and Blacks. His *First Family Foundation for Human Development* had been making a lot of noise lately. And his message and movement was drawing a lot of unwanted attention to the drug under world.

ZoeMan sat fuming as he watched the live broadcast. He hated American niggas, but even more he hated *smart* American negroes that kicked up dust and stirred the people. He wanted Arthur Cruz dead. But first he had to deal with BG.

ZoeMan turned the TV off and turned his attention to Frantz, who was viciously *eye-fucking* one of the young naked Haitian girls that ZoeMan had parading his home.

"Frantz, what do you have to tell me concerning our problem?"

Frantz knew exactly what had happened with the last attempt on BG's life, but he was not going to be the one to tell ZoeMan that they'd failed. So he quickly removed his phone and called Pepper and Feebie, within seconds the two-man Haitian killing crew was standing before him.

"What happened with BG?" Frantz asked.

Pepper, the bigger, uglier Haitian looked from his partner Feebie to Frantz and then to ZoeMan before speaking nervously. "Boss, we...we found the house and killed two men... but B, BG was not there."

"He was not there?" ZoeMan questioned, narrowing his big eyes.

"No-no, sir, boss," Pepper stuttered, rubbing the Voodoo beads that he always wore.

The man was an old school killer that truly believed in the power of the Voodoo. He wore the beads and made many sacrifices to the dark saints because he sincerely believed that they would always keep him safe.

"You killed two of his men?"

"Yes, boss."

ZoeMan trusted the big killer, he had never once let ZoeMan down. Pepper always got his man. ZoeMan did not believe as Pepper believed—in the Voodoo and hocus-pocus—however he did believe in the power of Pepper's trigger finger.

"You find him, Pepper! You find him and bring him back to me alive!" ZoeMan screamed.

"Yes, sir, boss."

ZoeMan dismissed them with the wave of a hand and turned his lusty attention to his teenage harem.

Chapter 12
Hot Pursuit

Detective Sims was just finishing up a meeting with some bigwigs from Homicide and the Drug Task Force. After the murders of Teddy P and 50, the Mayor went ballistic and put pressure on the Captain, who in turn chewed Detective Sims a new ass. The Mayor wanted BG, LG and every hoodlum associated with the vicious gangland killings off of the streets. Miami was his city, and his livelihood depended on tourist money—lots of it. He was not going to allow a gang of ignorant, insignificant, *nigger-thugs* to affect his finances.

Sims had life-sized photos of LG and BG, along with photos of four different murder crime scenes. There were also guns and large quantities of drugs that had been recovered. The file that cased all of the information was labeled LITTLE HAITI KIDS, even though the crew had ties in Carol City, Brown Sub, and Liberty City, their primary stumping grounds and home base was Little Haiti.

Detective Sims had given the men an exaggerated history on the brothers, adding murders that he knew they had absolutely nothing to do with. He passed photos of Doc's near decapitated body as he warned that the twins were "always armed and extremely dangerous."

¢ ¢ ¢

Lil One, LG, BG, and JackBoy were back *bottom-side* of the map. They rode by the Wynnwood address to find that the police were still everywhere. From there they went over to 36th Street. It was clear that someone knew their whereabouts and was telling ZoeMan their every move. The question was *who*?

When they made it to 36th Street, BG went left onto NW 2nd Avenue, heading back to Little Haiti, he just had to check out the hood. BG spotted Niko squatting on 53rd and pulled up next to him.

"What's up, kid?" BG greeted.

"I'm good... and you? Y'all kids really wildin' right now," Niko replied, not really wanting to be around BG. He knew all about the beef that was cooking between BG and V-Dub's crew, but now ZoeMan was involved and had a very attractive price on their heads—the hood was no place to be seen with BG.

"Y'all boys should be *ducked off*, 'cause Zoe pushin' contracts," Niko said.

"Niko, yo, fuck that *pussy-ass* nigga! We ain't runnin' from *nann* nigga, kid," LG yelled from the car's passenger seat.

"Yo, I ain't really trippin', kid, I fuck wit' y'all. I'm just sayin', though... Be careful."

"Oh, we're careful," LG stated, removing the towel from his lap and revealing the short Bin Laden style AK-47.

"Hit me if you hear anything, yo."

Niko agreed with the nod of his head and was happy to see BG and his crazy-ass brother drive the fuck off. Niko had a lot of love and respect for BG—as did the rest of the hood—but he wasn't ready to die with or for him.

BG pulled off and shot across 54th Street, coming down 3rd Avenue. He blew the horn at Bam and Ant as he passed them on the corner. The two looked as if they'd both seen a ghost. LG waved the AK-47 in a *real-nigga's* soldier salute. They waved back.

BG was on his *48 Laws of Power*. So much depended on reputation, *so guard it with your life*, and that's exactly what he was doing. He wanted everybody and their momma to see him riding hard in the hood, not running scared. Thereby raising his *gangsta* and making ZoeMan seem to be the vulnerable one. He was opening holes in ZoeMan's reputation.

As he sat at the light on 62nd Street and 2nd Avenue, shots erupted. *Tat! Tat! Tat! Tat! Tat!* The bullets ripped through the back window. Lil One and JackBoy got as low as they could while BG shot off through the red light. Lucky for them there were no oncoming cars. LG readied the AK and positioned himself to unload on the dark-colored sedan that sped up behind them.

Yyyyyyyaaaaaaaaaaaaaakkkkkkkk!!! a full clip emptied in seconds. LG quickly flipped the 37 round clip and prepared to empty again.

BG swung a wild left on 69th Street, trying to make it to I-95. By now, Lil One had his .40 out of the window dumping, *Doom! Doom! Doom! Doom! Doom! Doom!*

When BG hit the ramp to I-95 traffic was crawling. He side-swiped a candy-green *Donk* and hit the emergency lane. He had no choice but to jump back off of the expressway at the next exit...

¢ ¢ ¢

Pepper was hot on BG's ass. Feebie was hanging out of the window bussing as they exited on 79th Street and flew through the corner gas station at full speed. With all of the fast turns and cutting through traffic, it was very difficult for either of the shooters to get off a clean shot.

Bullets flew wild, striking buildings and other cars as they sped by. 79th Street was a busy six lane road that was always filled

133

with traffic. Storefronts, car lots, apartments and lots of small businesses littered both sides of the main drag. But that didn't stop BG and Pepper from engaging in their wild high-stakes game of cat and mouse.

"I can't get a good shot!" Feebie yelled, steady dumping at his target.

Pepper gritted his yellow teeth and gripped the steering wheel tighter. There was nothing more that he could do. BG was a NASCAR driver, taking corners at speeds of 40 mph. Pepper just hoped that BG would lose control and crash out.

BG had no intentions of crashing out as he sped down 81st Street going the wrong way. Cars were blowing their horns and veering off the road to avoid head-on collisions with the speeding cars that were sending lead back and forth at one another...

¢ ¢ ¢

Detective Sims sat in his unmarked patrol car, at the red light on 81st Street, eating a ham and cheese sandwich, when out of nowhere things went crazy. *Boom! Boom! Boom! Boom! Boom!* big guns echoed.

Detective Sims dropped his sandwich and ducked, thinking that someone was shooting at him. When he rose back up he could not believe his eyes. Two cars flew down 81st Street going the wrong way, exchanging gunfire.

"What in the hell?" Sims asked himself.

He immediately called in for backup as he hit his red dash-mounted light and got in pursuit. Speeding to catch up, Sims stayed on the radio calling in the play-by-play. He followed at a safe distance as the cars raced through Biscayne Plaza, still shooting. Listening to the heavy bangs of the shots, he knew that at least one of the shooters had an AK-47. He prayed that the son-of-a-bitch would soon run out of ammunition.

Now two additional police cars were trailing. "We need all available cars to get to 79th and Biscayne—suspects are westbound on 79th!" Sims yelled into his radio, hot on Pepper's tail.

¢ ¢ ¢

"Nigga, whip this bitch, we got *nine* on our ass!" LG yelled, still *licking* the AK at Pepper's car.

Shit was *all-the-way* crazy now. More patrol cars were joining the chase. LG knew that it wouldn't be long before the *ghetto-bird* swooped in.

"Man, just do whatchu do, bruh, I got this..." BG said calmly and continued pushing the rental car to the limit. Working the rearview mirror and his side mirrors, he was able to see everything going on behind him as well as keep his eyes on the road ahead. That's why most high-speed chases ended in a wreck-out—the driver would turn his head looking behind him.

He saw the police coming in larger numbers. Time was not on his side, he had to do something quick to evade the killers and the cops.

LG was almost out of clips and he hadn't scratched the driver or the shooter. As BG flew down the avenue and tore through someone's fence, LG took slow deliberate aim and squeezed off three rapid shots. *Yak! Yak! Yak!* Feebie was struck dead-center of his chest, and went flying from the window from which he hung. His body hit the asphalt with a bounce and was met by the bumper of Sims' car.

¢ ¢ ¢

"Fuck!" Pepper yelled as he saw his friend and long time partner fly from the window. He immediately lifted his MT-90 from the seat and opened fire. *Ffffffffrrrrrrrr!!!* the handheld mini-assault rifle fired, tearing the back of BG's rental up.

Pepper had the pedal to the floor, hoping to get side-by-side with BG's car. But BG kept weaving in and out of the lanes, slamming against other cars.

BG then made a wicked left on NW 2nd Avenue. Pepper attempted to follow but because he was firing his gun and only had one hand on the wheel he didn't make it. *Boom!* he slammed into the building that sat on the corner. Had it not been for the airbags Pepper would've died on impact. Instead, he jumped out of the passenger side window, gun still in hand, and fled the scene.

¢ ¢ ¢

BG peeped in his rearview mirror just in time to see his pursuer crash into the building. A small wave of relief rushed through him. Now his only issue was to shake the *poe-poe*. Flying past 71st he made a right on 69th Street, and then a left on 3rd Avenue. He slammed on brakes and everybody jumped out running. Jumping over two gates and back through a backyard, they came out in Steve's yard. Steve was standing out front with Rah-Rah.

"Damn, kid, what the fuck?" Rah-Rah said upon seeing them run up.

JackBoy was scared and out of breath. "Nah, yo... the car... gotta wipe it down."

BG, LG, Lil One, JackBoy and Steve went inside of Steve's crib while Rah-Rah took a crack-head with him to get the car in order. LG got on the phone and called Shara to come and get them. BG was shook. Every time he heard something he ran to the window. JackBoy was in the corner mad as hell. He'd had his head down through the whole gunfight—not firing his gun once.

"Y'all boys are 54, yo," Rah-Rah said, coming back from handling the car. "Ain't no police nowhere."

BG and the crew were happy, but surprised to hear that.

¢ ¢ ¢

Pepper had the MT-90 in his hand as the squad car came around the corner. He had two choices, run and possibly be shot in the back, or stand his ground and die with his boots on. Pepper chose the latter, letting the small but powerful gun talk.

Ffffffffffrrrrrrrrrrrr!!! the MT-90 ripped off into the police car. The officer stopped and tried to reverse, but Pepper was now running towards him, gun still spraying. *Ffffffffrrrrrrr!!!* the MT-90 held 130 rounds of .40 caliber bullets. At least 67 of those rounds were now deeply embedded in the policeman's face, chest and rear seat of the squad car—after running clean through the officer.

Pepper quickly turned, seeing a white woman in a gold Mercedes truck. He walked up to the car and pointed his weapon. The scared woman quickly ducked, trying to avoid an early meeting with her Maker. Pepper snatched the door open and barked, "Bitch, get yo' cracka-ass outta the car before I kill you!"

Without a moment's hesitation the woman jumped from the car, landing on her face and chest. Pepper jumped in and slowly drove off down the street, passing Detective Sims as they both turned the corner of 2nd Avenue.

¢ ¢ ¢

Detective Sims heard a lot of rapid gunfire as he neared 2nd Avenue. He slipped his .9mm from its holster and proceeded with caution. After passing a gold Mercedes truck on the corner of 2nd Avenue, what Sims saw made him sick to his stomach. A police squad car riddled to pieces, the officer inside was shot up worse than the car. His blood and brains covered every inch of the car's interior. The poor fool who had sworn to serve and protect had been served—*dead*.

"Calm down, Miss, please...tell me what happened here?"

The lady finally calmed herself enough to explain, in great detail, what she'd seen and experienced at the hands of the horrible black man. Sims looked in the direction of the gold truck he'd just passed and felt his blood boil. As he stood there with the woman, police cars began pouring in from everywhere.

"Now you guys show up!" Sims shouted loudly.

Detective Sims led the car-jacking victim to the rear of a police cruiser where an officer could take her statement. Then he got on his own radio and placed an APB out on the stolen truck. Deep down inside Sims knew that BG and LG were somehow involved in this whole mess. It was all over the streets that they were at war with ZoeMan.

"Let me see how you explain this one, Detective."

Sims turned to find Captain Williams staring down at him.

"Oh, no, you can't put this one on me, Captain Williams."

"I'll put it wherever I see fit, Detective. The Mayor is on my ass, and I'm on yours. Now get me an arrest! I don't care who it is, but get me an arrest! If I get anymore heat from this... by God, it'll be your ass that cooks... not mine."

"I understand, Captain," Sims said and walked away wanting to kill BG, LG, and Captain Williams.

¢ ¢ ¢

After all that had happened that day, BG and the gang made it back up to Palm Beach with Hot Rod and his crew. They all sat around drinking and smoking weed while Hot Rod watched the events from earlier on his 50" TV. The news had a full recap of everything that had happened. Hot Rod couldn't believe the damage that his new partners had caused, and walked away from without getting killed or going to jail.

"Y'all bitches is crazy! The two of y'all is like Bo and Luke Duke," Hot Rod said laughing.

BG looked puzzled. "Who the fuck is Bo and Luke Duke, kid?"

LG laughed and shook his head. He didn't know who the fuck Bo and Luke Duke were either, and really he didn't give a fuck. He was just happy to be free, fuck being alive. Because he would rather have died today than to have been arrested. To him life was not worth having if you could not live it the way you wanted.

The twins had sold Hot Rod three kilos when they came back. LG was now in the process of whipping up another one for 6th Street. They were about to get their grind on in a major way.

"Man, this old-ass baking soda is fuckin' up my *whip-game*, kid," LG yelled from the kitchen.

"Nah, bruh, yo' ass just can't cook," BG shot back.

Everyone bussed out laughing at LG.

"Yo' wrist ain't proper like mine, kid," JackBoy added, still laughing.

"Whatever, just hurry up. I'm tryna hit Ocean Eleven, so we can play some pool, my nigga," Hot Rod said.

Once LG was finished they stopped on 6th Street to drop some work off and headed over to the pool hall to gamble and drink.

¢ ¢ ¢

"Hello, Detective Sims, please."

"This is Detective Sims, is this Miss Jones?"

"Yes, it is... I need to talk to you."

Keisha had some information for Detective Sims concerning BG and LG's whereabouts. She had ran into Muffin—Missy's cousin—and Muffin told her where she could find them. Muffin was Shara's best friend, so Shara had mentioned where LG was in a casual conversation. She had no idea that talking to Muffin

139

would in turn hurt LG, just as Muffin had no idea that her sharing the conversation would ultimately hurt Shara.

Detective Sims was totally surprised by the call. "So what is it, Miss Jones?"

"He's in West Palm Beach, both of 'em."

"Are you one hundred percent sure?"

"Yes, I'm sure. I also heard that the shoot-out on the news involved him and his brutha, that's why they left Miami."

Detective Sims was elated. This information would definitely get his ass out of the fire, and possibly get him that promotion he wanted so desperately.

"Miss Jones, if all goes well I'll need you to testify to a grand jury and possibly in court... You won't have anything to worry about because he will be behind bars. Him and his entire crew... And when it's all over I'll have the government to move you and your children to a big pretty house wherever you would like to live."

"Anywhere?" Keisha asked.

"Anywhere."

"And you will have *all* of my charges dropped?"

"What char—" Sims caught himself. He'd forgotten about the false charges that he'd lied to her about. "What charges wouldn't I drop, huh? You have been very cooperative; I will have *all* of them thrown out for you, okay?"

Keisha was still under the impression that she was actually being charged for something. The bullshit that Sims had ran on her really had her shook. She was now grateful.

"Thank you, Detective, thank you so much. And if I hear anything else, I'll call."

"You do that and have a pleasant day."

Sims hung up the phone and turned to one of his co-workers, laughing. Keisha had been on speaker phone and Detective Lee had overheard the entire conversation.

"For crying out loud, how stupid can that girl be? She hasn't been charged with anything," Lee said, laughing with Sims.

"Man, I scared the shit out of her stupid black-ass."

The two sat and shared some more laughter at Keisha's expense.

Chapter 13
The Setup

Sunny was at home, broke, wondering where his next *stack* was coming from. It had been a minute since he'd heard anything from JackBoy or Nut. He sort of felt like his entire plan was going to ruins. He'd come too damn far to just let everything go down the drain.

"What in the hell I'ma do now?" Sunny asked himself.

That's when it all hit him. All he had to do was cut out the middle men and go straight to the source, ZoeMan. He was more than sure that ZoeMan would pay top dollar for good firsthand information. First he had to get out and get some information to tell. Sunny decided right then and there that he would no longer be playing both sides. He was going to play for one side… *the big money side*… ZoeMan's side.

"Sunny, why you ain't been thought of this from the get go?" he spoke to himself.

He didn't answer himself because he still had a problem. Once he got the information, how was he going to get it to ZoeMan? He could always send word, but he wanted to tell the boss man himself, to get full credit for the information.

"I'll just go and squat up at Cezar's," he concluded.

Cezar's was a barbershop and hair salon that sat in Little Haiti on 59ᵗʰ and NW 2ⁿᵈ Avenue. Sunny knew that all of the big time Haitian bosses hung out there. He would just stop and post up until the boss of all bosses came through. He had nothing to lose and everything to gain. Sunny rushed to his car and sped off to jump start his foolproof plan...

¢ ¢ ¢

Sunny sat in Cezar's parking lot calming his nerves. This was to be his moment of truth. Sunny snuffed out the Newport butt he'd been smoking and took a deep breath. He then exited his *big-boy* BMW 745I. It was his pride and joy, next to his condo and Platinum Rolex, it was his biggest purchase.

If one were to merely look at Sunny they would think that he was a millionaire twice over and going again. While the truth was, Sunny was two late payments from skid row—simply flossing for the moment.

When Sunny reached the door to Cezar's, he hit the buzzer and waited. Because so many big time Haitian bosses and their women frequented the establishment, security was always tight. You couldn't just walk in, you had to be buzzed in by one of the barbers.

Cezar's unisex salon had a beauty salon in the front—always filled with dime pieces looking to increase their beauty or their bank—while the barbershop was to the left and in the back. Sunny greeted the ladies as he made his way to the back. All eyes were on him the minute he entered the barber's area. An older Haitian man sat in the corner, surrounded by a group of younger, stronger Haitians. They all stared as Sunny came in sporting his thug apparel, which older Haitians hated.

"How can I help you, sir?" asked Cezar, the owner of the shop. He'd only buzzed Sunny in because he thought that Sunny was there to pick up one of the ladies.

"Oh, umm, I need to speak with ZoeMan."

All of the men in the barbershop looked at each other as if to say, "What the fuck does this low level thug want with the boss?" They then turned their glances to Sunny like, "Never heard of him."

Cezar spoke what everyone was thinking. "I'm sorry, friend, we don't know anyone by that name."

Sunny had expected them to say some shit like that. Of course, he wasn't going to give up that easy. He pressed on. "Look, sir, I have some information for him concerning V-Dub."

The room filled with tension when a big, black, ugly Haitian stood up. "And who are you, sir? What is your name?" he asked in his heavy accent.

Sunny nervously looked up at the 6'8", 265 pound giant. He'd never died before, but after looking at what stood before him, Sunny was positive that death had to look just like him. He began to stutter, "Sssunny," while his brain was telling him to run.

The giant began approaching Sunny.

Sunny almost pissed on himself when Pepper slapped his big hand on his shoulder and said, "come." Leading Sunny outside with two other men following them. Without one word being spoken the four men got into a black Volvo and drove off.

Sunny stared out of the window as they rode down North Miami Avenue. He had absolutely no idea where they were headed. He only prayed that he would survive the ride. All of a sudden his foolproof plan didn't seem so foolproof.

The Volvo came to a stop in El Portel, at a house on 93rd Street. "Come, we'll go inside," Pepper said and led the way.

Once again Sunny followed the giant. And the two quiet henchmen followed Sunny. His mind raced as they cleared the double doors, entering the house. As soon as they were inside and the doors were locked, a blow was thrown and Sunny's lights went out. The man that hit him with the baton stood over his unconscious body and drew back to strike Sunny again, but Pepper stopped him.

Pepper then whipped out his phone to call the boss.

"Hello?" ZoeMan answered.

"Boss, I have something..." Pepper went on to tell ZoeMan about Sunny.

After hearing all that Pepper had to say, ZoeMan had Frantz to ready the car. ZoeMan wanted to see Sunny for himself and hear firsthand what he had to say.

¢ ¢ ¢

"Hell nah, kid!" BG yelled after Hot Rod three-railed the eight ball and sunk it in the left corner pocket.

That made the third straight game that Hot Rod had cooked BG, and they'd all ended with a vicious trick shot. Of course, it was all in fun and games. BG and his squad, along with Hot Rod and his men, were just hanging loose and having fun at Ocean Eleven. JackBoy's cell phone went off. It was the new love of his life.

"Aye, y'all boys quiet down. This my baby, China Doll," JackBoy said, all *happy-go-lucky*.

"Man, make that bitch sweat some, yo!" LG said, fucking with his man.

"Whatever, nigga!" JackBoy answered. "What's up, China?"

"Hey, JackBoy, what's goin' on?"

JackBoy walked off to a corner booth and put his *mack* down. He really wanted to see China Doll, but she was playing shy with him, knowing damn well she wanted to see him, too. She knew that JackBoy wasn't just paid, he was laid—she had felt his enormous penis during the lap dance she had given him.

"So what's up, baby?" JackBoy popped. "Let's do a movie and dinner."

"Boy, no. Un-uh. You can't take me to no movie and dinner. I don't know you like that," she said sternly, but playfully.

145

"Okay, well, look. Let me be your dinner instead, and we can make a movie… if you want to," JackBoy capped back.

"See!" China Doll laughed. "I knew yo' ass was crazy."

"Only 'bout my baby-momma… China, you tryna be a millionaire?"

China continued to laugh and JackBoy continued to run his game. But for real, it wasn't game. It was the truth, JackBoy was really digging her and couldn't understand what a perfect dime with such a cool personality was doing shaking her ass in the strip club. Of course, he was not judging her, he was feeling her.

"Look, lil' momma, stop playin' wit' a real nigga. Let me come through."

"I told you that yo' ass was crazy."

"Girl, why you actin'?"

"Actin'?"

"Yeah, actin'! Frontin' like you ain't feelin' the kid. It's a million and one females in the Palm Beach area tryna swallow young money and you fakin' like you ain't hungry… Man, I'm through wit' the lil' girl mind games, I'm gone."

JackBoy took the phone from his ear and was about to hit end when China Doll stopped the games.

"Boy, wait!" she yelled.

"For what?"

"For me to give you my address… Are you happy now?" China Doll said with a slight attitude.

"Why you make a nigga go through all of that?"

"Boy, are we goin' to the hotel or not?" she asked simply.

A big-ass Kool-Aid smile spread across JackBoy's face. Right when he was about to throw in his hand, China Doll had agreed to go to the hotel with him. He didn't waste anymore time with the small talk. He wrote down her address with the quickness and hung up before she could change her mind.

It didn't take JackBoy long to finesse the keys from LG, find China Doll's house, and hit the first hotel on Blue Heron Blvd.

JackBoy couldn't believe how pretty China Doll was. She looked extra sophisticated in her long black trench coat, black stilettos, and her silky black hair up in a bun.

After paying for the room, JackBoy went right up and rolled four nice blunts of the finest weed Little Haiti had to offer. He fired one up, hit it twice, and passed it to China. She hit it and immediately began to gag. Laughing, he pulled out a big Ziploc of colorful pills.

"Here, lil' momma, this might be more ya speed," he said, passing China the bag of pills and taking the weed from her. He'd already taken two and a half pills before picking her up.

"Boy, is you tryna get me fucked up?" she asked, smiling as she removed two pills and popped them.

JackBoy smiled, he was feeling it. "I need you to keep up wit' me... 'cause I'm in the air, lil' baby, and I ain't comin' down."

China Doll stood up and removed her coat.

"Damn!" JackBoy let escape from his drooling mouth. China had on nothing but her stilettos and a pair of pink lace panties. Her bare breasts were firm and alert. JackBoy's dick quickly rose to attention.

"Wait right here, baby," China chimed and disappeared to the bathroom.

JackBoy placed his Glock .40 under the pillow and laid back. The pills had him right and he couldn't wait to taste China's pussy. So *fuck it*, he thought and came up out of his clothes.

China came back out of the bathroom butt booty-ass naked and rolling. She had her eyes locked on JackBoy's rock-hard dick. Smiling, she reached out and grabbed it... held it... admiring its thickness. The mere thought of her sucking him off caused his nature to jerk in her delicate hand. China took that as her cue and kissed the head... licked the bottom side of the shaft... and just as she took the full length of him into her hot, moist mouth and began to deliver the pressure, JackBoy heard a noise. He looked to the door and saw the knob slowly turn. With his focus no longer on China's *brains,* JackBoy reached beneath the pillow for his gun. He didn't want to admit it to himself, but he realized that this whole night was a fucking setup.

China Doll seemed to be really into administering *boss-fellatio,* but sensed a problem when JackBoy's penis began to soften in her mouth. "Bay," she asked, looking up. "What's wrong?"

The hotel room door opened just as the words left her mouth and JackBoy had his .40 out and aimed...

¢ ¢ ¢

A thundering punch to Sunny's *midsection* woke him up. The pain that the blow caused made poor cowardly Sunny see blue stars and pink clovers. But once he regained focus he saw death again. He was tied to a chair in a dark room with Pepper staring down on him. The only light in the room came from a crack in the door that emitted light from the hallway.

The back of Sunny's head was pounding from the shellacking with the baton. His only thoughts were of life, while his reality was certain death.

"What do you want me to do with him?" Pepper asked.

"Let me talk with him."

Sunny recognized Pepper's voice—it was dark and deep. However he could not make out the voice of the second man. Though it wasn't as aggressive as Pepper's hard voice, he knew that it was a voice of higher authority.

The unknown man pulled a chair up and sat down in front of Sunny. The man's face was sort of a blur in the darkness, though Sunny could see that he was a rather fat man.

"Now," the man began in his heavy Haitian accent. "Before I have you killed, why were you looking for me?"

"Mmmm, mmm," Sunny tried to say.

ZoeMan laughed and signaled for Pepper to remove the duct tape from Sunny's mouth. Sunny breathed deeply and licked his lips.

"I, I know the men who killed your nephew, sir."

"Tell me what you know!"

Sunny quickly did what he did best—spilled his yellow guts about everything he knew surrounding V-Dub's untimely demise. ZoeMan had already known most of the things that Sunny told him. Still, he listened.

"Sir, I can help you catch them...V-Dub was my friend." Sunny cried real tears.

ZoeMan really did want to catch his nephew's killers. So Sunny had his full attention. Of course, ZoeMan was a smart man, which caused him to remain a bit cautious as to Sunny's true motives. But not so cautious that he would ignore help finding BG.

"I don't need you!" ZoeMan yelled, still playing hardball.

"Bu-but, but..." Sunny stuttered. He was truly scared shitless. He'd never before in life been down this bad.

"But nothing! Maybe you are trying to set me up. Maybe you're really their friend."

"No, no...I promise! You can ask Nut. Ask him."

ZoeMan stared at Sunny evilly. Something about the scared young punk turned his stomach. Still, he removed his phone and called Nut.

"You better be telling the truth," said Frantz from the corner of the dark room.

When Nut answered the phone ZoeMan questioned him about Sunny. He never told Nut exactly what was going on. Yet once it was established that Sunny was indeed the Sunny that he claimed to be, ZoeMan told Nut to hurry over to the house on 93rd. Nut had been to the house many times before with V-Dub.

"Don't take long!"

"I'm out the door now, Zoe."

ZoeMan hung up the phone and walked over to Frantz. Sunny could hear the whispers, but could not make out what was being said. Sunny also noticed just how many men were spread out in the dark room. He was in deep shit and he knew it. His mouth and greed had finally gotten him killed.

About 30 minutes passed before a new man entered the room. Sunny lifted his head and stared wide-eyed at Nut coming through the door.

"Do you know this man?" ZoeMan asked Nut.

Nut was totally shocked at the sight of Sunny tied up to the chair. He did not know why Sunny was there in such a predicament. Or better yet, *why was he here being questioned about him?* Nut wasn't sure whether he should answer ZoeMan's question truthfully or not.

"Umm, ye-yeah. That's Sunny," he finally answered, already regretting the words.

Nut's answer sparked some hope in Sunny. "I told you I knew him."

"Hold up, Zoe, what's this all about, Unc'?" asked a scared Nut.

ZoeMan sat back down in his chair and explained everything to Nut as it was told to him. When he finished he turned to Pepper. "Let him go."

"You sure, boss?" Pepper questioned.

But after ZoeMan shot him an evil-eye he quickly untied Sunny and stepped aside. His insides boiled. He was very unhappy about what took place between him and BG. BG was still alive while his best friend and partner, Feebie, lay dead.

ZoeMan eyed the little coward as he was being untied, and realized that only money could motivate a man as scary as Sunny to do something so stupid.

"Sunny, you find me some good information and you report it to Nut. Nut will report it to me and you will be rewarded handsomely. Deal?"

"Yes sir, Zoe. I will do whatever I have to do," Sunny answered.

His plan had panned all the way out. It didn't start out as smooth as he would have liked, but wasn't it the ends that justified the means?

¢ ¢ ¢

"You stupid muthafucka!" Nut yelled as soon as the two were in his car.

Nut was not happy at all about the situation. For all he knew, he could've gotten killed. He cursed Sunny the whole ride to Cezar's to pick up his car. Calling the man all sorts of *bitches and pussy-niggas*. Sunny just rode along, not saying anything in response. His mind was made up, he'd made a major move today and not even Nut could change that.

Sunny got out of Nut's car 38 hot. He'd taken it, but he was not cool with the way Nut was talking to him. Of course, he was too much of a bitch to say anything about it.

"Who the fuck you think you talkin' to? Nigga, I gotta trick for yo' hoe-ass!" Sunny finally got the nuts to snap back. But only after he was in his own car and sure that Nut could not hear him.

Sunny thought hard on his way home. He was going to make Nut pay for disrespecting him. "Stick a fork in that nigga, 'cause he's done, huh? For flappin' his tongue, huh?" Sunny quoted a verse from one of Juvy's songs.

He planned to get Nut killed and also get closer to ZoeMan. Sunny was a quick and clever thinker, so he knew just what to do and who to use to get it done.

¢ ¢ ¢

JackBoy was already out of the bed and on his feet when the door swung all the way open. He was just about to tap the hair-trigger

151

on the Glock .40 when the cleaning lady stepped into clear view. Seeing the naked man aiming the big-ass gun at her, the Spanish woman fell to her knees and began yelling, "I sorry! I sorry! Por favor no me mates! I sorry!"

She was supposed to be cleaning room 223, but had entered room 222 by mistake. A mistake that almost cost her her life.

JackBoy quickly lowered his gun and pulled on his jeans. He then ran over to the lady and handed her three, one-hundred dollar bills. He apologized for pointing the gun at her. She shook her head and left.

"Oh-my-God," China Doll cried out.

She'd been hiding under the covers the entire time. She was just as scared as the maid had been. The look in JackBoy's eyes, combined with the size of the gun he held, really freaked her out.

JackBoy didn't give a fuck. He thought it was going down. "That bitch almost made me kill both of y'all hoes."

"Both of us?" China Doll asked in shock.

"You heard me. You think I was gon' shoot her and not you?"

China Doll all of a sudden realized exactly what type of dude she was dealing with and how he thought. JackBoy thought that she had set him up. China couldn't believe that he thought so low of her. She was hurt.

"Look, I'm just gon' get my things and leave," she said, standing.

She was ass-naked and looking good enough to eat. JackBoy's nature started to slowly rise. He could not allow her to leave, not like this.

"Hold up, lil' momma... wait." He grabbed her and hugged her around the waist. They were both still nude, and the pills that they'd popped earlier had their senses and emotions on edge. When the flesh of their abdomens touched, feelings of pure ecstasy exploded throughout their bodies. "I'm sorry, ma... Don't go. A nigga really 'bout that life, ya heard me? So what a nigga s'posed to think? We just met and the door swings open on us in a

152

hotel you picked? Come on, ma..." JackBoy whispered in her ear, holding her. His erection was pressed on her stomach.

China Doll didn't respond verbally. She fell back onto the bed and positioned herself to be entered from behind. JackBoy smiled wickedly as he looked at all of that pussy and ass waiting for him to have his way with it.

He climbed on the bed and entered her. "Mmmm!" China moaned, her vaginal walls wrapped tightly around his long, thick shaft. Her pussy was much better than he had anticipated... Long, tender strokes. China loved every inch of him... She was a real pain-freak, so she threw it back at him hard, wanting it to go as deep as her stomach.

"Ooooh, boy!" she managed to say.

She had her face buried in a pillow while JackBoy had 10" of dick implanted in her gushing vagina. China pulled and tore at the bed sheets with every thrust. She loved it.

JackBoy looked down to see her melted ice cream covering his shaft. Seeing the way that it leaked onto him and dripped to the bed sheets only made him pound her longer and harder... faster... deeper... "Oh, JackBoy, oh... God!"

The drugs had them both on cloud nine. The air conditioner was on high, but the room still felt hot and sticky. The smell of China's sex and strawberry lotion filled the air and became stronger as she had her orgasm.

"Ooooh, baby, baby, please?!" she yelled. "Let me turn over, bay."

China lay on her back and put one of her legs behind her head.

JackBoy could not believe what he was seeing. China's fat, wet pussy sat up like prime-steak stacked on a butcher's block. JackBoy went in, driving his stiletto in and out of her swollen raw flesh. China met his aggression by grabbing hold of his ass and pulling him down faster. He tried to keep up, but his nature would no longer allow.

153

"Oh, China, baby, a nigga cummin'!" And he exploded.

The two lay silent for a while.

"Are we gon' have a round two?" China asked.

"Shiid, round two must gon' be on you," JackBoy replied, thinking that China was trying to get some money out of him.

"Nigga, round one, two, and three are all on me... This wasn't 'bout no business, JackBoy, this was pleasure."

JackBoy smiled, he really did like her. "See, China, I ain't even want this to happen to you."

"Boy, whatchu talkin' 'bout?"

"You done fell in love wit' the dick."

China bussed out laughing. JackBoy was good people in her eyes and she planned to enjoy him for however long he would allow her to.

Chapter 14
The Double Cross

Nut and his wifey Keisha had just left the 163rd Street mall when Nut got a call from snake-ass Sunny. Sunny told him that he had something very important to tell him. Nut agreed to meet him in Carol City at the Race Trac gas station on 167th Street and 27th Avenue.

Nut jumped on the 826 Expressway heading west, towards the 27th Avenue exit. Keisha was on the passenger side playing her position. She could care less where Nut was going as long as she was there with him.

"Damn, girl, slow down," Nut said, laughing.

Keisha rolled her eyes and continued to crush her Big Mac, milkshake and fries. "Boy, don't watch me, watch the road."

Nut laughed and continued to watch her eat. She was a very pretty girl and lately she'd been adding a few pounds in all of the right places.

"Yo' ass is gon' buss that seatbelt. Keep eatin' all that fast food," Nut joked, still staring at her as he drove.

"Whatever, boy... but you need to watch the road, Nut!" Keisha screamed at him.

She had been a little moody lately, but Nut should have known better. Keisha always wore her seatbelt and moved carefully in vehicles, because she had lost her mother in a deadly car accident. Keisha promised herself that she would not die in a car.

As Nut approached the exit, he hit the turn signal and got off the 826 on 167th Street and 27th Avenue. He could see the gas station, but he didn't see Sunny's car. *Where the fuck is this sucka-ass nigga?* he asked himself, mad that Sunny was not in place. Nut grabbed his phone and dialed Sunny's number.

"Yeah?"

"Yeah my ass, where the fuck you at? I ain't got time to be fuckin' 'round wit' you."

"Come on, big homie, that's my bad. I'm leavin' outta Carol Mart right now," Sunny pleaded with Nut.

"Nigga, hurry yo' ass up!"

Nut hung up the phone fuming. He made up his mind right then and there that Sunny was dead. As soon as he got the information and confirmed BG's demise, he was going to kill Sunny himself.

¢ ¢ ¢

BG and LG were back in Miami on business. They were the only two that came down. JackBoy was still somewhere *ducked off* with China Doll and could not be reached. They had called his phone many times and kept getting the voicemail. Lil One was running tough with Hot Rod and holding the fort down on 6th Street.

LG's lungs were full of weed smoke and his evil eyes were low. He and BG had been smoking all day. Well, at least LG had. BG merely puffed and passed. He had a lot on his mind and really was not in the mood to get high. There was murder in the air. So he needed to be one hundred percent focused.

"You think this shit one *hu'nid*, bruh?" LG asked, taking the blunt back from BG. "'Cause this shit done travelled through a lotta lips."

"I don't know, bruh… Let's just hope it is."

The two were referring to some information that LG had received from Shara, who had gotten it from talking-ass Pooh, who got it from fuck-ass Sunny.

"Nah, Sunny's chin-ass better hope it is," LG said in a deadly tone.

BG pulled the car into the Winn Dixie parking lot on 168th Street and 27th Avenue, right across from the Race Trac gas station. There the two brothers waited for a call from Sunny.

"Where this nigga at?"

"Yo' guess is as good as mine, bruh. This is where he said he would be. But for real, we out here bad, sittin' here in this parking lot."

There were three weapons in the car—.357, AK and a MAC-11—so they were strapped and ready for whatever. Neither man trusted Sunny, yet they had to play along to his tune if they wanted their man.

BG's phone rang. "Yeah, what up?"

"BG, he's at the Race Trac in a black Rover," Sunny whispered into the phone.

BG didn't say one word. He slammed the car in gear and shot out into traffic. The Range Rover was parked at pump #15. BG pulled down his ski mask and scanned the busy street for police cars. Seeing none, he slow-rolled up next to Nut's SUV. Before Nut could peep the play, both brothers were out of the car shooting, *Tat! Tat! Tat! Tat! Tat!* the MAC-11 sounded, shattering the rear window.

Boom! Boom! Boom! Boom! Boom! the AK riddled the expensive truck.

BG was now point-blank range on the driver's side window. The shooting ceased. BG opened the driver's door and almost went into shock. "Nah, hell nah, man!" he cried out.

LG heard his brother's words and quickly snatched open the passenger side door. His mind raced, thinking that maybe it wasn't Nut in the vehicle. Of course, Nut was dead... but Keisha was also in the vehicle, bleeding, but still breathing.

Her pretty eyes were open. Blood leaked from a wound in her chest area and dripped from her trembling lips. She looked at BG and reached her hand out to him. "Help," she whispered.

"Keisha, damn," BG said sadly and reached out for her hand. "LG, man hel—"

Boom! a shot sounded.

BG ducked quickly and upped his MAC-11. It was then that he realized the shot had come from his brother's gun. "Why the fuck did you do that?" he yelled.

LG didn't say a word. His response was, *Boom! Boom!* He fired two final shots into Keisha and Nut's body. He turned and raced back to the car. BG could hear sirens sounding in the distance. He took one last glance at Keisha and ran off behind his brother.

Keisha was dead. She died in a car, just like her mother... Only hers was no accident, it was a double-cross.

¢ ¢ ¢

The news report was all over the TV concerning the brutal double-homicide that had taken place at the Race Trac gas station. Everybody from the Mayor's office, down to the NAACP was on the news expressing their concerns and their contempt for the senseless violence. Even Arthur Cruz and his First Family Foundation were on the scene denouncing the ignorant black-on-black violence. The black community was in an uproar!

The fact that Keisha, a mother of two, had been killed was bad, but the fact that her unborn child was murdered before it even had a chance to experience life angered people.

When BG saw the news he felt like shit. For the first time in his life he was mad and not speaking to his brother.

Of course, LG didn't give a fuck about Keisha or her dead child. He loved BG, but his being mad about the incident with Keisha's death didn't move him one bit. People fell-out all of the time, he just figured that it was their time. Sooner or later, BG would realize that he had done the right thing. There was absolutely no way that they could have just taken Keisha to the hospital and trusted her not to tell. Whatever BG was thinking, he had LG fucked up.

They still had business that needed to be handled, so they were forced to be around one another. Hot Rod did not know the details surrounding their problem, but he could see that it was really bothering BG.

"My nigga, you straight?"

"Yeah, I'm aiight, dog... I'm good," BG answered Hot Rod.

Hot Rod had been spending a lot of time around the twins and he knew that BG was not himself. So he turned to LG for answers.

"Man, that nigga trippin' 'bout that bitch!" LG yelled.

"Fuck you, nigga! You didn't have to shoot her... Man, she was pregnant! Stupid-ass nigga, we killed a baby!"

"Soft-ass nigga, you're pussy 'bout that bitch! Fuck her and the baby she was carrying. That shit ain't no pressure on me. Not none! Lord knows I stay high and when I get to hell, Lord knows I'm gon' fry." LG laughed in his brother's face.

BG was now in his feelings. He rushed over to LG, but Hot Rod stepped in between them. LG was still laughing.

"Come on, BG... You gotta chill, dog."

BG pushed Hot Rod aside and stormed out of the front door.

Once in his car, he sped off. Heading down Blue Heron Blvd, his state of mind at this point was "Fuck LG!" He didn't need him. The truth was, he knew that he was wrong and that he would always need his younger brother—just as his younger brother would always need him. Pride would not let him turn around and patch things up.

BG hit I-95 South, headed towards Miami. He blasted Tupac's *Me Against the World* as he drove.

Chapter 15
The Fall Out

Detective Sims sat in his office throwing darts at a picture of BG and LG. Sims knew where to find them, thanks to Keisha. He had no authority in Palm Beach, and he was unwilling to contact the authorities in Palm Beach. No, they would not climb the ladder of success off of his hardwork. Sims would simply wait until they returned to Dade County. He knew they would, they always do.

"I'm gonna get you two," Sims said out loud.

It was about time for Detective Sims to take his lunch break, he was hungry and very agitated. He grabbed his coat and caught the elevater to the lobby, thinking about what he would eat. *Red Lobster… Sizzler… Burger King…* he questioned his belly as he jumped into his car and headed to a nearby greasy-spoon. Before he could reach the *hole-in-the-wall* restaurant, his phone began to ring.

"Detective Sims," he simply answered.

"Hello, Detective Sims," the caller replied.

"Yes, who's calling?"

The mystery caller told the detective about a problem that "they both shared" and made him an offer that he could not refuse.

It was 8:00 p.m. and BG still had not returned. LG was mad at his brother, but he was also worried. He, along with Lil One, Hot Rod, and JackBoy were on the way to Miami. He knew that BG had gone back down and he didn't want him there alone.

"You tried his phone?"

"Yeah, 'bout a hun'id times! He got the shit turned off," LG answered Lil One. "Get off on 69ᵗʰ Street, yo."

Lil One caught the exit, heading towards Steve's house. LG hoped that BG was over there chilling and not out in the open.

When they hit Steve's block it looked like a party. All of the homies were out—Steve, Rah-Rah, Mono, Niko, Kim, T-Girl and an old friend of BG and LG, TrapCity. LG looked around at all of the different faces before getting out of the car. There were a lot of faces that he did not recognize.

Everyone got out of the car except Lil One. He stayed behind with the AR-15.

"Speakin' of the devil," Niko said.

He had not seen LG or BG since the day that they had stopped by the park on 53ʳᵈ and got into that big shoot out and high-speed chase. They were just talking about the incident when LG and his crew pulled up.

"Fool, why y'all forever rappin' 'bout a nigga?" LG asked, laughing.

"Shiid, stop doin' crazy shit for us to rap about," Rah-Rah capped back.

Everyone laughed together before LG introduced Hot Rod to all of his Little Haiti homeboys. He and Steve walked over to the side of the house, where they could not be seen by any passersby.

"How y'all boys been?" Steve asked sincerely.

"Shiid, *gettin' it how we live*, kid."

"I heard about Nut... Where's BG?"

LG just shook his head and let Steve put two and two together. Steve knew how the twins got down. They got it just how they lived—hard!

"Well, look, kid, you need to be with him. Shit lookin' crazy and this ain't no time for the bullshit."

LG knew that his big homie was right, but in his eyes, he'd only done what he was programmed to do. He wondered where his brother was. He wished that this whole beef-shit would never have taken place. All he wanted was for his big brother and cousin to come home from jail, so that they could get money together.

The sound of gunshots in the distance broke LG's train of thought. He immediately thought of BG. Could it be BG being shot at?

LG ran to the car with Hot Rod and JackBoy hot on his trail. When they made it to the car Lil One was already behind the wheel and ready to whip. They sped off in the direction of the shots.

"Damn, I hope that ain't my brutha," LG said aloud.

He then said a quick silent prayer as he dialed BG's phone, there was still no answer.

By the time they made it to 56th Street the shots had ceased. Still, Lil One continued to ride the area, searching for the location the shots had come from.

"Yo, go by Sunny's crib, he might have seen BG around there."

They were on 4th Avenue. Sunny lived right over on 5th Avenue. Rounding the corner, they saw Sunny standing in front of his house talking to someone in a black BMW 745LI with dark tinted windows. Lil One whipped up next to the car. LG cracked his window just enough for Sunny to see it was him.

"Sunny, check this out, yo."

Seeing LG had Sunny's eyes wide and scared shitless. He did not know what to do. Walk over and talk to LG or continue talking to Frantz, who had no idea that LG was parked in the rental because of the dark tints.

"What's up, homie?" Sunny asked weakly, and made his way over. His whole body was shaking like a naked stripper on ice.

LG looked at the sneaky little Haitian. "You know where them shots came from?"

"Man," Sunny began. "That shit was crazy. That was dumb-ass Seal or Loon, I'm not sure what he's callin' himself these days."

Everybody in the car laughed at Sunny's sly wit. The shit wasn't really funny, it was more of a relief. LG was glad to hear that BG was in no way involved with the shooting. Still, he needed to find him.

"Aiight then, Sunny, I'll have that for you tomorrow, yo."

LG was referring to the $10,000 that he and BG had agreed to pay Sunny for setting Nut up.

"Aiight, kid, tomorrow."

LG rolled up the window and Lil One pulled off.

¢ ¢ ¢

"Y'all ain't see how kid was actin' funny?" asked JackBoy after they were back in traffic.

He had been watching Sunny's movements, and noticed that he was nervous about something. The question was *what?*

"I peeped that shit, too," agreed Hot Rod.

LG thought about the two comments from his friends and reflected back on the conversation he'd had with Sunny. His body language did seem a bit peculiar.

"Y'all might be right. I wonder who the fuck was in that BMW?" LG thought hard. Where had he seen that BMW before? He knew for certain that he recognized that car. He remembered mostly the *big-boy* kit that was on it. "Man, we gon' follow that shit."

164

LG had Lil One hit the park on 53rd Street, where they located Homie Joe and Dre sipping from large white cups. Rushing, LG jumped out of the car, still holding his gun.

"Nigga, lay down!" a voice yelled from the cut.

LG stopped dead in his tracks, only realizing then that he'd gotten out of the car with his gun in a heavy drug area. Everybody around the park was buying drugs, selling drugs, watching out for the drug dealers, or holding the guns to protect the drugs.

Laying the gun down on the sidewalk, LG raised his hands. "Nah, homie, I'm good. Joe and Dre are my niggas... Yo, Homie Joe! Dre!" LG yelled.

The two hood-bosses looked over and saw their young gunner holding Gemo's little cousin at gunpoint. Homie Joe quickly waved his shooter off and told LG to pick up his gun.

As fast as he could, without putting Joe and Dre too far in his gameroom, LG explained his situation. Dre and Homie Joe were very good friends of Gemo, so they agreed to loan LG a car.

Dre waved a sexy little black-bone over to him and whispered something in her ear. She ran off, and when she returned, she was in a gold S600 Mercedes with limo tints.

"I know it's some shit that you ain't tellin' us," Dre said, handing LG the keys. "But this is Gemo's car, if you fuck it up, that's yo' ass."

Everybody hopped out of the rental and got in the clean 600. Lil One took the wheel again and they were off.

"Right on muthafuckin' time!" Hot Rod said, seeing the BMW pull away from Sunny's crib.

As they drove by Sunny's house in pursuit of the BMW, LG saw Sunny going back inside. "I'll be back to see you if this shit ain't right," he said to himself. He wished like hell that BG was right there riding with him. He needed him, but they had fallen out.

Chapter 16
Nap Him

The BMW got on I-95 North, heading towards 62nd Street. Lil One made sure he stayed a few car lengths away, so that he would not alert the driver of the 745. While riding, LG continued to think, he knew with great certainty that he'd seen that BMW before. *Where? Where? Where?* He wrecked his brain. Just as he was about to succumb to defeat, it hit him like a ton of bricks!

"Oh, shit, that's ZoeMan's shit!" he yelled.

He knew right then that Sunny's bitch-ass had been up to no good the whole time. Of course, he knew that ZoeMan would never personally fuck with a lowlife crab like Sunny, therefore it had to be either Frantz or ZoeMan's other henchmen that they were following.

LG took his strap off of safety and smiled. The opportunity to end this whole war was now in his hands. Or they would at least go up a piece—killing ZoeMan's right-hand man would be equivalent to capturing an opponent's Queen in chess.

"Let's ride up beside that nigga and blow his whole shit up!" JackBoy said angrily.

Everybody in the car waited to see what LG had to say.

He leaned back in the plush leather of the 600 and rubbed his chin. *What would bruh do?* he thought before answering. "Nah, we gon' *nap* the nigga."

"Like a dirt-nap?" Hot Rod asked.

"In due time, Rod. For now, I mean kidnap the nigga."

Hot Rod could not believe his ears, kidnapping was an automatic life sentence. LG was proving to be crazier than he had thought. Nevertheless, Hot Rod was with him.

¢ ¢ ¢

The BMW jumped off of I-95 at the 95th Street exit. Lil One was right behind him. When the light changed the BMW pulled into the BP gas station. Seeing Frantz get out of the vehicle made LG want to snatch him right then and there. There were too many witnesses at the gas station, and 95th Street was a very busy street.

LG could not just sit there, though. "Rod, he don't know you, go in there and buy somethin'. While you in there, rap wit' the nigga."

Hot Rod got out and went into the store while LG hopped out and ran over to the BMW. He tried the door and it was open. He quickly slid into the backseat and got low.

About three minutes later, Frantz came out and began pumping gas, he waved at Hot Rod as he passed en route to the car.

"Where's LG?" he asked. He never saw LG get out of the car.

"That crazy-ass nigga in that BMW up there," JackBoy said, smiling, he loved the way LG always did the unexpected.

Frantz finally finished pumping his gas and got back in the car. Lil One had already pulled off and busted a quick U-turn. He needed to see which way Frantz was going.

"What the fuck he doin'?" asked Lil One, seeing the BMW's break lights light up.

The car turned off on to a dark side street. Lil One floored the Benz...

¢ ¢ ¢

That night Detective Sims sat in his car at Denny's on 36th Street near the airport, waiting on his mystery caller to show up. Sims had agreed to meet the man so that they could talk business—neither man trusted the phone lines. It was now 10:36 p.m. and the maverick detective was starting to worry. *Where in Sam's hell is this guy?* Sims wondered, he was now 36 minutes late.

"I don't have time for this shit, I could be at home with my wife," Detective Sims soliloquized.

Frustrated, he started the car and was just about to pull off. His actions were halted by the ringing of his phone. The phone's display read *unknown caller*. It was the mystery man.

"Where are you?"

"In the parking lot."

Sims looked around and found the statement very hard to believe because he had not seen any cars come or go in the last 15 minutes.

"In the parking lot, where?"

"Across from you, about two spaces over."

Detective Sims looked over and spotted a Dodge Nitro. Sure that that was his man, the detective checked his service revolver and began walking over. He looked around twice and got in. To his surprise, Sims found a very large gun to his head.

"Don't move or you are a dead pig!" one of three men said. "Get his fuckin' gun!"

The driver reached over and took the gun off of Detective Sims' waist. The men then pulled off. Sims was sweating bullets. He never thought he'd find himself in this position. All of the wrong that he had done over the years as a dirty cop flashed through his mind. He knew that death was promised to everyone,

168

yet he didn't want his to come like this—at the hands of some lowlife nigger, *street-punks*.

¢ ¢ ¢

LG had his arm around Frantz's neck with his gun to his head. Seeing bright lights flood the small dark street, LG looked in the rearview mirror and saw the gold 600 coming. Hot Rod and JackBoy both jumped out and went into action. Frantz was quickly checked for weapons and pistol-whipped with the .45. All Frantz could do was cover his bleeding face and hope that Hot Rod would stop hitting him.

Frantz was then thrown in the backseat of the car with LG and JackBoy flanking him.

"Nigga, put yo' head between yo' legs and keep it there!" LG demanded.

Hot Rod took the wheel and whipped off in a hurry, not sure if anyone had witnessed the brutal kidnapping. Lil One followed close behind.

Within seconds they were southbound on the perfect escape route—I-95. Lil One was not sure what LG's plans were or if the young fool even had one at all. He quickly called him up.

"What's up?"

"Whatchu doin', bruh?"

To Lil One's surprise, LG already had his next move mapped out. "We 'bout to snatch Sunny's bitch-ass."

"What?"

"Just trust me, yo. We gon' get this beef shit over, bruh... tonight!"

"Whatever, bruh, I'm witchu," Lil One slurred. "We *gon' get it how we live*, fool."

LG hung up and tried calling BG again, still no answer. LG really needed his brother on this one, but even without him, he had to *get it how he lived*.

169

"Where we headed?" Hot Rod asked from the driver's seat.

After hearing LG's response Hot Rod sighed heavily. Why were they going to Sunny's house? Hot Rod immediately expressed his concerns with that idea. How were they just going to pull up in Little Haiti in Frantz's BMW?

LG thought for a minute. "You're right... Go to the Subs."

"Where?"

"Just stay on I-95 'til you get to the 836, then jump off on 22nd Avenue."

Lil One was from Brown Sub, so LG knew that he could easily get them a fresh set of wheels or a spot to lay low for a while.

When they pulled up they were greeted by a pleasant surprise.

"There's BG right there!" Hot Rod pointed after spotting BG's rental.

BG, on the other hand, saw the black BMW coming his way and automatically thought that it was a hit. He jumped off the hood of the rental car and reached for his *strap*. His man Var was with him and they were both ready for a gunfight.

Before any cannons could explode Hot Rod lowered his window and began flashing his headlights.

"Hold up, BG, it's us, my nigga!" Hot Rod yelled.

"Damn, what's up, Rod?" asked a confused BG.

By then Lil One had pulled up and walked over to the car. Hot Rod lowered the rear window for BG to peep the lick, all he saw was LG and JackBoy. Then he looked a little closer, noticing a dude with his head tucked between his legs.

"We got that nigga Frantz," LG said before his brother could figure it out, then told him about everying that had happened.

BG could not believe his eyes or ears. He looked at the man still in the crash position, looked at his brother and then to Lil One.

170

"Bruh, yo' brutha's a dog wit' it. Nappin' niggas is my thang and I couldn't have done it any better," Lil One said, twisting his short dreads.

Var could not believe it either. He knew that Frantz was a *big-boy* in every sense of the phrase. "What y'all gon' do now?" he asked.

BG thought for a minute and then laid it down. "Put Frantz's bitch-ass on hold for now. I'ma need you to stay here Var and watch the nigga. The rest of y'all, we goin' to get Sunny."

¢ ¢ ¢

The kidnappers had Detective Sims in the parking lot of a local strip club called the Pink Pussy Cat. After making sure that they had not been followed, one of the kidnappers placed a call. "Yes, we have him," was all that he said.

In about 30 minutes a car pulled up. Sims watched as a man approached the car that he was being held in. The man was very well dressed and moved with a confident swagger. Once he got to the car, all of the men in the Dodge Nitro exited, giving the man one-on-one privacy with the captive.

"Mr. Sims, I am sorry for your inconvenience, but I really needed to speak with you alone."

Before Sims responded he looked out of the window and noticed the three men were standing guard. "What is this all about?"

The man smiled, his teeth were pearly white and even. "It's about a problem we both share...BG and LG...You heard of them?"

Detective Sims breathed a sigh of relief. He thought for certain that his past misdeeds had caught up with him and that his wicked life was going to end on this night. However, hearing BG's name, he knew that was not the case.

"Yeah, I'm a cop. Of course I have heard of them."

ZoeMan thought for a moment, he was no longer smiling. "BG and his brutha killed my nephew and I want them dead... Can you help me?"

"Can I help you? I'm a frickin' cop!" Detective Sims was totally baffled. He'd killed many men for high paying drug lords, but who was this guy? "Who sent you and what is your name?"

"Captain Williams and Lewis are very good friends of mine."

"Are you ZoeMan?"

"Yes, I am. Please, let's go somewhere and finish our discussion."

ZoeMan took Detective Sims to one of the docks that he owned on the Miami River. They boarded his cargo boat. There were 2,500 kilos of cocaine on it. The men sat down and enjoyed a nice Haitian meal and drank some fine Haitian Rum as ZoeMan explained what he needed done.

"So what do I get?" Sims asked.

"$15,000 a month, plus $150,000 for handling the BG problem."

"Deal," Sims agreed.

"Good."

The two men shook hands to seal the deal and out came a smiling Captain Lewis.

"I told you we could trust him, Zoe," Captain Lewis stated and poured himself a drink.

¢ ¢ ¢

The crew was out in front of Sunny's crib blowing the horn. Sunny looked out of the window and saw that it was BG. *I hope this nigga ain't 'round here on no sucka shit,* he said to himself and went outside.

"I got that cash for ya, kid," BG said from the driver's seat.

Sunny broke out into a Kool-Aid smile. "Bet!"

"Ain't shit, kid... Ride wit' us right quick. We need another favor," LG said.

Sunny did not hesitate. He had money on his mind. Plus they needed a favor, which only meant more money. "Where we headed, kid?"

"We just gon' ride and look for a minute."

The rest of the crew was in the car following them as they rode and talked.

"Yeah, kid, the chick that was with Nut was pregnant... Shit all over the news," Sunny stated.

"Oh, yeah?" BG responded, acting as if he had not seen the news report for himself.

Sunny went on and on, adding his own version. They were back in Brown Sub before they knew it. That's when Sunny noticed Var leaning on Frantz's black BMW. In a panic he tried to jump out of the car, but BG had the child-safety lock on the rear doors.

"Nah, Sunny, where you tryna go, kid?" LG said as he hit Sunny in the head with his pistol.

When the two brothers drug Sunny's semi-conscious body from the car, they followed Var into the house. Frantz was gagged and tied to a chair.

"You gotta iron in here?" LG asked.

"Yeah, it's one 'round here somewhere."

"Get it, I gotta old-school Lil Haiti trick I wanna show y'all boys."

BG and JackBoy were shaking their heads. They already knew what it was. They'd seen some super thugged out niggas piss and shit on themselves when that iron hit them. Before it was all over they would be willing to tell on their own mommas.

Sunny must have witnessed it also, because when LG approached him with the hot iron in hand, Sunny started crying and begging.

"LG! BG! Please, I was gon' set them up for y'all! Like I did with Nut. I swear to God, please!" Sunny screamed like a bitch.

BG stuck a dirty sock in Sunny's mouth, and then placed duct tape over it. LG hit him in the chest with the iron.

"Mmmmmmm!!!" Sunny tried to scream as his eyes bucked and his flesh sizzled. The aroma of pork roast filled the room.

Large beads of sweat popped up on Frantz's face. He knew he was next in line for the hot iron. He jerked at the tape that bound him to the chair, but it was useless.

"Damn," JackBoy said. "Most niggas would have passed out by now. Sunny, you're a tough nigga."

LG was thinking the same thing, so he took the iron off of Sunny's chest, removing a large portion of flesh. He then pressed the iron to the side of Sunny's face. Sunny jerked twice and passed out from the pain.

LG nodded to JackBoy for him to remove the tape from Frantz's mouth.

"Look, I ain't gon' play no games witcha *chin-ass*. You got one chance to come clean or end up like yo' boy over there," LG stated matter of factly.

Frantz got straight to the point. He told them everything that he knew regarding ZoeMan—places of business, hang outs, his bitch's crib, and where he laid his head.

With all of the information that Frantz had given them, killing ZoeMan would be like child's play. They were planning to rob his ass as well.

BG ran down the plan. If it worked out as smooth as BG had explained, they would all be rich by sunrise.

"Well, it sho' as hell sounds easy enough," said Hot Rod.

"Looks like you're comin' along for the ride, kid," BG said to Frantz before upping his .40. *Boom! Boom!* he fingered the gun, shooting Frantz in both legs. "We don't need no trouble outta you durin' the ride."

"What's up wit' this nigga?" Var asked, pointing at Sunny.

174

"Shiid, kill 'im."

Without a word, Var pulled his gun and *Boom*! He shot Sunny point-blank in the face.

¢ ¢ ¢

ZoeMan, Detective Sims and Captain Lewis were having a great time smoking Cuban cigars and drinking Haitian Rum. ZoeMan wore a bright smile on his face, while inside he frowned a thousand frowns. He despised the two skunks that sat before him. Not only were they crooked white devils, but they were police—a fundamental instrument of oppression. Be that as it may, he needed their kind to stay on top. He deemed his compromise as a part of business, nothing more and nothing less.

Detective Sims was a bit tipsy and talking like a radio announcer. He told ZoeMan all about his encounters with the twins and how he suspected that they'd killed his informant, Keisha.

"These two could really be a problem for us," said Captain Lewis.

What he really meant was "a problem for them." Captain Jeffrey Lewis was a master at shifting weight and passing the buck. He really didn't give a shit whether they ever caught or killed the twins. His sole purpose for getting Sims and ZoeMan together was to get ZoeMan off of his own back. True enough, he knew that Sims was a dirty cop that could possibly handle the job of killing the twins, but if he failed, it was he and ZoeMan's problem. When the Mayor started bitching again, he would simply bitch to Sims—shift weight and pass the buck. All of the pressure was on Sims.

"Boss," Pepper said, entering the room. "Frantz still has not answered his phone."

Frantz was supposed to be at this meeting because it was his job to deal with scum like Detective Sims. ZoeMan only dealt with the Captain and higher-ups.

"Good help is so hard to find," said a frustrated ZoeMan. "Keep trying and don't come back until you reach him!"

Pepper headed back to the top deck to smoke a blunt. *Fuck ZoeMan and Frantz,* he thought. Calling Frantz was not a part of his job description.

Sims looked at Pepper's wide back as he departed. "That's one big, scary looking man," he said, pouring another shot of rum.

Chapter 17
Out Manned & Out Gunned

The squad rushed back to 53rd Street to return the Benz and jump back into the rental. They made their way over to 68th to *holla* at Rah-Rah and the crew. The only real firepower that they had was the AR-15, they needed more for what they were about to attempt. The men pulled over on the block, followed by the black BMW. LG got out to *holla* at Mono, Rah-Rah, and Steve.

"Check it, yo," LG said excitedly. "I need some *sticks*, yo."

"Say no more, yo," Rah-Rah replied.

He left and returned with a small duffle bag. Inside were two Mac-90's, an AK-47, and two Mini-14's.

LG thanked them and jumped back in the car. He rode in the rental with Hot Rod, BG and a tied up Frantz, while Lil One and JackBoy were in the 745. Everybody's mind raced as they neared the docks.

"Th-th-that's th-the boat ri-right there." Frantz pointed out, he'd lost a lot of blood and looked awful.

They sat and watched the large boat for a while. There was no movement. "They gotta be on the lower deck... let's move out," LG gave the order like a seasoned commando.

The squad was split up into two groups. BG and Hot Rod crept low to the ground, moving in from the south as Lil One, LG and JackBoy entered the boat.

"If it's breathin', kill it," Lil One said.

The trio was now at the point of no return. Venturning deeper, they scanned the huge vessel for any movement. No one said a word. Their only means to communicate were hand signals. Once they reached the lower deck, they heard laughter coming from the inside. Carefully they made their way...

¢ ¢ ¢

Captain Lewis had had enough of ZoeMan and Detective Sims' company for the night, and was preparing to leave. When out of nowhere they heard a shot go off, *Boom!*

"What the—" was all Sims got to say before he looked and noticed that Captain Lewis had been *dome-called.* "Oh my God!" he yelled and ran for cover.

Lewis was stretched out dead in a pool of his own blood.

Pop! Pop! Pop! Pop! Pop! Sims fired from his hiding spot.

Boom! Boom! Boom! Boom! Boom! Boom! Boom! Boom! the return fire came tearing up the cabin.

Sims ducked back into his safety spot and found that ZoeMan had joined him. The big Haitian boss was curled into a fetal position with his hands covering his ears.

"Just my fucking luck!" Detective Sims said to himself and began searching for a way out.

¢ ¢ ¢

Pepper smiled a devious smile, because he was in perfect position to kill all three of them. But before he realized it someone else was also bussing a gun. He just wanted to get a little closer... closer... and things went wrong. The three shooters suddenly split

178

up. One went to each side and one up the middle. Pepper chose his target and fired, *Tat! Tat!* He smiled as the man fell dead in the center of the room.

¢ ¢ ¢

BG and Hot Rod were just boarding when the shots began to ring out loudly. They moved as fast as possible, without leaving themselves open, to join the gunfight. The two men covered each other's blind side as they moved. BG was the first to go in.

Boom! Boom! Boom! Boom! gunfire continued to erupt.

Coming down the small stairwell that led to the lower deck, BG saw a man taking aim at Lil One, he wasted no time, *Yak! Yak! Yak! Yak!* All four rounds found their intended target, leaving Pepper dead where he stood.

¢ ¢ ¢

Lil One saw JackBoy's head explode seconds after they split up. In a panic he turned, but it was too late. The ugly giant had him covered. He quickly said a prayer and braced himself for the bullet's impact. Instead, the giant's chest exploded before him, and the large man collapsed. BG was standing in the stairwell with a smoking AK-47 in his grasp. Lil One thanked God and rushed over to JackBoy, but there was nothing he could do for him... He was gone. Hopefully with the good Lord.

¢ ¢ ¢

Bullets were flying all around the small cabin. ZoeMan was still in his fetal position. *Where is Pepper, where is he?* he asked as Detective Sims emptied another clip and quickly slammed another in. He had to give it to the detective; he had nuts, because whoever was onboard clearly had them out gunned. ZoeMan

179

drew the courage to sit up. Bullets were steady flying and he knew it would not be long before Sims was either killed or ran out of bullets. ZoeMan looked around for a way out, because when either of those predicaments presented itself, he wanted to be long gone.

¢ ¢ ¢

"Shit!" Detective Sims said aloud.

He was out of bullets and could hear the gunmen slowly advancing on him. He thought about Captain Lewis' gun, but his dead body lay too far away. There would be two dead bodies if he went for that gun.

"Well, well, well," Sims heard a familiar voice say.

When he looked up he found LG staring down at him.

"I'm a cop, you can't kill me."

"No, you're a *crooked* cop."

"No, no, no, son. You have this all wrong! We were making a drug bust."

LG had to laugh at that. He was fully aware that the detective worked homicide not drug task.

BG walked over and saw the dirty *shit-for-brains* policeman trying to explain himself and snapped. He slammed Sims in the chest with the stock of his AK-47 and snatched him up by his bushy salt and pepper hair. Sims was pulled over to where JackBoy's dead body lay.

"You see him, cracka? That's my main man right there!" BG yelled.

Boom! was the next and the last sound that the detective heard.

Tat! Tat! two more shots sounded from across the room. It was Hot Rod putting Frantz to rest.

BG now had ZoeMan in his grasp, asking him where the cash and drugs were. Before ZoeMan could answer Lil One yelled,

180

"Jackpot!" He'd found the mother lode. It was all boxed up in one hundred percent Colombian Blend coffee boxes.

"Look, my friend, there is—" ZoeMan began to beg, but was silenced by BG's AK blast, *Yak! Yak!* And his lights were out...

¢ ¢ ¢

The crew loaded up as many boxes as they could. BG wanted to take everything, but there was only so much that they could fit into two cars. Had they known, they would have driven an eighteen wheeler.

The men were working hard and fast tyring to *get-it* and *get-gone*; when Lil One looked up and spotted trouble. "Oh, shit!"

About four sets of headlights were moving at a high speed, coming directly at them. Because ZoeMan owned this particular dock, the men fastly approaching were not your ordinary *rent-a-cop* security.

Boom! Boom! Boom! Boom! Boom! Boom! Boom! Boom! Boom! Boom! the men quickly got off, seeing that Lil One already had his gun in hand.

Hot Rod, BG and LG all scrambled to get their weapons, but the advancing troops were simply coming too hard.

Boom! Boom! Boom! Boom! Boom Boom! Boom! Boom! shots exploded and levitated Hot Rod, pinioning his lifeless body to a metal cargo box. He died with his eyes open.

Yyyyyyyyyaaaaaaaaaaakkkkkkkkkk!!!! BG unloaded a full fifty round clip into the lead car, stopping it in its tracks.

The sight of Hot Rod plastered to the cargo container with his chest and stomach ripped open sent the twins into Rambo mode.

LG ran at breakneck speed to the other side of the huge metal container and began to buss off like a madman, *Yak! Yak! Yak! Yak! Yak! Yak! Yak!*

They were both holed up in a good position to cover their asses and pick up the oncoming killers. Neither man could locate their partner, Lil One. There was no sign of him. "Damn, I hope Lil One ain't dead," BG said as he continued to fire.

LG could see BG out of his peripheral vision. He was deeply entrenched in the gunfight. Muzzle flashes lit up the whole area as automatics bussed repeatedly. The sound was deafening. LG knew deep down that this would be the last time that he took the battlefield with his brother, but he was not afraid. He only hoped that BG would be the one to make it.

By now the men in the remaining three cars were out of their cars and taking position. There were eight men in total, and probably many more en route. If BG and his two man army couldn't end this fracas within the next minute or so, they were as good as dead. Lil One knew this. He was pinned down bad, but willing to sacrifice himself to save the twins. The gunmen were bunkered down near a gas tanker. Everytime he raised up rapid fire sent him back into hiding. As if on cue, the twins went in for one last hurrah, *Yyyyyyyyyyyyyaaaaaaaaaaaaaaaakkkkkkkkkkkk!!!!* They unloaded and the gunners turned their full attention to combat them. Lil One used this opportunity to run out in the open and squeeze off two good shots, *Boom! Boom!* And the tanker went up in flames, *BOOM!!!*

The three friends hurriedly got into their cars and hauled ass before the police arrived.

To Be Continued In:

GET IT HOW YOU LIVE: Volume 2WO:
The Hostile Takeover

Order it now on amazon.com or go to badlandpub.com

BADLAND PUBLISHING LLC
PO Box 11623
Riviera Beach, FL 33419-1623
www.badlandpub.com

Shipping address

Name:_____

Address:_____

City:_____State:_____ Zip:_____

Title	Author	Price
STREET RAISED: The Beginning	Mike Harper	15.95
BOO BABY: The Secret Of…	PLEX	15.95
SERVED: With No Regard!	PLEX	15.95
STREET RAISED: The Raw Deal	PLEX	15.95
BUCKIN' DA' DICE Vol. 1	BOOK GANG	15.95
NO TURNING…	Big Nation	13.95
PROMISCUOUS	Calvin Williams	10.95
SUGAR	Mike Harper	15.00
CRUMBS TO BRICKS	Capo Cat	15.95
GET IT HOW YOU LIVE Vol. 1	Big Gemo	13.95
GET IT HOW YOU LIVE Vol. 2	PLEX & Big Gemo	14.95
GET IT HOW YOU LIVE Vol. 3	PLEX	14.95
LOVE & THUGGIN	Bo Brown	15.00
EROTIC DESIRES	Seven Supreme	13.95
LIL ONE: Blood Investment	K-1 & Bino	15.00
ONE LOVE	PLEX	13.95
sOmEtHiNg 2 DiE 4	PLEX	14.95
YOUNG-N-THUGGIN	Troy Jones & PLEX	14.95

3.75 (S&H) for 1-3 Books _____
For Quantities over 3 add $ .75 per Book   _____

PLEX PRESENTS:

GET IT HOW YOU LIVE

Volume 3hree

PLEX

Erotic Desires

By Seven Supreme & The Book Gang

sOmEThInG 2 DiE 4

A Classic Novel
By PLEX